THE
SNOW
SPIDER

THE SNOW SPIDER

THE MAGICIAN TRILOGY

BOOK ONE

JENNY NIMMO

ORCHARD BOOKS

AN IMPRINT OF SCHOLASTIC INC.

NEW YORK

LIBRARY OF CONGRESS CATALOGING-IN-PUBLICATION DATA AVAILABLE
ISBN 0-439-84675-7
10 9 8 7 6 5 4 3 2 1   06 07 08 09 10

Printed in the U.S.A. 23
First Scholastic edition, September 2006

Cover illustration by Brandon Dorman
Text type set in 14-pt. Garamond 3
The display type was set in Dalliance Roman
Book design by Marijka Kostiw

For David

CONTENTS

THE
SNOW
SPIDER

CHAPTER ONE

The Five Gifts

GWYN'S GRANDMOTHER GAVE HIM FIVE GIFTS FOR HIS BIRTH-day, his ninth birthday. They were very unusual gifts, and if Gwyn had not been the kind of boy he was, he might have been disappointed.

"Happy Birthday!" said his grandmother, turning her basket upside down.

Gwyn stared at the objects on the kitchen floor, none of them wrapped in bright birthday paper: a piece of seaweed, a yellow scarf, a tin whistle, a twisted metal brooch, and a small, bro-ken horse.

"Thank you, Nain!" said Gwyn, calling his grandmother the name she liked best.

"Time to find out if you are a magician, Gwydion Gwyn!" said Nain.

"A magician?" Gwyn inquired.

"Time to remember your ancestors: Math, Lord of Gwynedd, Gwydion, and Gilfaethwy!"

"Who?"

"The magicians, boy! They lived here, in these mountains,

maybe a thousand years ago, and they could do anything they wanted, turn men into eagles and soldiers into dust; they could make dreams come true, and so perhaps can you!"

On special occasions Nain often said peculiar things. Gwyn could not think of a reply.

"There has been an ache in this house since your sister went," said Nain, "the ache of emptiness. You need help. If you have inherited the power of Gwydion you can use it to get your heart's desire." She turned on her heel. "I won't stay for dinner!"

"We've only just had breakfast, Nain!"

"Nevertheless . . ." She swept away, down the hallway and through the open front door, her black hair sparkling in the golden mist that hung over the garden, her dress as gaudy as the autumn flowers crowding by the gate. Then she looked back and sang out, "Give them to the wind, Gwydion Gwyn, one by one, and you'll see!"

Gwyn took the gifts up to his bedroom and laid them on the windowsill. They looked like the most improbable effects for a magician.

"What is she going on about?" He scratched his uncombed hair. From his tiny attic window he could see Nain's dark head bobbing down the mountain track. "She travels too fast for a grandmother," Gwyn muttered. "If my ancestors were magicians, does that make her a magician, too?"

His father's voice roared up the stairs. "Have you fed the chickens, Gwyn? It's Saturday. What about the gate? The sheep will be in the garden again. Was that your grandmother? Why didn't she stay?"

Gwyn answered none of these questions. He gathered Nain's gifts together, put them in a drawer, and went downstairs. His father was outside, shouting at the cows now, as he drove them down the track to pasture.

Gwyn sighed and pulled on his boots. His grandmother had delayed him, but she had remembered his birthday. His father did not wish to remember. There was no rest on Saturday for Gwyn. No time for soccer matches, no bicycle to ride down to the town. He was the only help his father had on the farm, and weekends were days for catching up with all the work he had missed during the week.

He tried not to think of Bethan, his sister, as he scattered corn for the hens, and searched for eggs in the barn. But when he went to examine the gate, he could not forget.

Beyond the vivid autumn daisies, there was a cluster of white flowers nestling beneath the stone wall. Bethan had brought them up from the woods and planted them there, safe against the winds that tore across the mountain. Perhaps, even then, she had known that one day she would be gone, and wanted to leave something for them to remember her by.

"Gwyn, I have something for you." His mother was leaning out of the kitchen window.

"Dad says I have to fix the gate!"

"Do it later — it's your birthday, Gwyn. Come and see what I've got for you!"

Gwyn dropped his toolbox and ran inside.

"I just wrapped it," his mother apologized. "Did Nain bring you something?"

"Yes. I thought everyone else had forgotten."

"Of course not. I was so busy last night, I couldn't find the paper. Here you are!" His mother held out something very small, wrapped in shiny green paper.

Gwyn took the present, noticing that the paper had gold stars on it.

"I chose the paper especially for you." Mrs. Griffiths smiled anxiously.

"Wow!" Gwyn had torn off the paper and a black watch was revealed in a transparent plastic box. Replacing the numbers, tiny silver moons encircled the dark face of the watch, and as Gwyn moved it, the hands sparkled like shooting stars.

"Oh, thanks, Mom!" Gwyn clasped the box to his chest and flung his free arm around his mother's neck.

"It's from us both, Gwyn. Your dad and me!"

"Yes, Mom," Gwyn said, though he knew his mother had not spoken the truth. His father did not give him gifts.

"I knew you'd like it; you're always looking at the stars, you funny boy. Take care of it now!"

"Of course I will. It's the kind of present for a magician. It's like the things Nain gave me."

His mother drew away from him. "What things? What do you mean, a magician? Has Nain been talking nonsense again?"

"Come and see!" Gwyn led his mother up to the attic and opened his top drawer. "There!" He pointed to Nain's gifts.

Mrs. Griffiths frowned at the five objects lying in a row on Gwyn's white school shirt. "Whatever is she going on about now? I wish she wouldn't do such things." She picked up the broken horse and turned it over in her hands.

"It has no ears, Mom," Gwyn remarked, "and no tail. Why did she give me a broken horse?"

"Goodness knows!" His mother held the horse closer and peered at a tiny label tied around its neck. "It's in Welsh," she said, "but it's not your grandmother's writing. It's so faint. *'Dim hon!'* I think that's what it says. 'Not this!'"

"What does it mean, Mom? 'Not this!'? Why did she give it to me if I'm not supposed to use it?"

His mother shook her head. "I never know why Nain does things."

"She said it was time to see if I was a magician, like my ancestors."

"Don't pay too much attention to your grandmother," Mrs. Griffiths said wearily. "She's getting old and she dreams."

"Her hair is black," Gwyn reminded her.

"Her hair is black, but her eyes don't see things the way they used to!" Mom picked up the yellow scarf. "This, too? Did Nain bring this?"

"Yes. It's Bethan's, isn't it?"

His mother frowned. "It disappeared with her. She must have been wearing it the night she went, but the police found nothing the next morning, nothing at all. How strange! If Nain found it, why didn't she say so?" She held the scarf close to her face.

"You can smell the flowers," said Gwyn. "Do you remember? She used to dry the roses and put them in her clothes."

His mother laid the scarf back in the drawer. "Don't talk about Bethan now, Gwyn," she said.

"Why not, Mom? We should talk about her. She left on my birthday. She might come back . . . if we think of her."

"She won't come back! Don't you understand, Gwyn? We searched for days. The police searched, not only here, but everywhere. It was four years ago!" His mother turned away, then said more kindly, "I've asked Alun Lloyd to come over for your birthday. We'll have a proper party today, not like your other birthdays. You'd better get on with your work now."

When Mrs. Griffiths left the room, Gwyn lifted the scarf out of the drawer and pressed it to his face. The scent of roses was still strong. Bethan seemed very near. How good she had looked in her yellow scarf, with her dark hair and her red raincoat, all bright and shining. He remembered now: She had been wearing the scarf that night — the night she climbed the mountain and never came back. Why had Nain kept it secret all this time, and given it to him now, on his birthday?

"If Bethan left her scarf," Gwyn exclaimed aloud, "perhaps she meant to come back."

He laid the scarf over the broken horse, the seaweed, the whistle, and the brooch, and gently closed the drawer. He was humming cheerfully to himself when he went out into the garden again.

❄ ❄ ❄

Mom kept her word. Alun Lloyd arrived at four o'clock. But he had brought his twin brothers with him, which was not part of the arrangement.

There were nine Lloyds all crammed into a farmhouse only one room larger than the Griffithses', and sometimes Mrs. Lloyd, always eager to acquire a little more space, took it upon herself to send three or four children, when only one had been invited. She was, however, prepared to pay for these few precious hours of peace. Alun, Gareth, and Siôn had each brought a gift, and Mrs. Griffiths, guessing the outcome of her invitation, had provided a party for seven.

Kneeling on the kitchen floor, Gwyn tore the colored paper off his presents. A red kite, a pen, and a pair of black plastic spectacles with a large pink nose, black eyebrows, and a black mustache attached were revealed.

"Looks like your dad, doesn't it?" giggled Siôn, and he snatched up the spectacles, put them on, and began to prance up and down the room, chest out and fingers tucked behind imaginary suspenders.

Suddenly it was like other people's birthdays. The way a birthday should be, but Gwyn's never was.

Nain arrived with a box under her arm. "For your birthday," she said. "Records, I don't want them anymore."

"But you gave me your presents, Nain," said Gwyn.

"Don't look a gift horse in the mouth," Nain retorted. "Who are these nice little boys?"

"You know who they are. The Lloyds, Alun and Gareth and Siôn, from Tŷ Llŷr. Don't you ever see your neighbors?" chided Gwyn.

"Not the one with the glasses — I don't know that one. Looks like your father." Nain chuckled. "Put on some music, Glenys!"

"Well, I don't know. . . ." Mrs. Griffiths looked worried. "Ivor put the record player away; we haven't used it since . . ."

"Time to get it out then," said Nain.

Somewhat reluctantly, Mrs. Griffiths knelt in a corner of the kitchen and, from a small neglected cupboard, withdrew the record player. She placed it on the kitchen table while the boys gathered around.

"I can't remember where to plug it in," said Mrs. Griffiths.

"The light, Mom," Gwyn explained. "Look, the plug is for the light."

"But . . . it's beginning to get dark." His mother sounded almost afraid.

"Candles! We can have candles!" Gwyn began to feel ridiculously elated. He got a box of candles from the pantry and began to set them up on saucers and bottles all around the room.

Then they put on one of Nain's records. It was very cheery and very loud: a fiddle, a flute, a harp, and a singer. The sort of music that makes you go wild, and the Lloyds went wild. They drummed on the table, jumped on the chairs, stamped on the floor, waved the dishcloths, and juggled the cat.

Nain began to dance in her purple dress and black lace stockings, her dark curls bouncing and her colored beads flying. She wore silver bracelets, too, that jangled when she raised her arms, and a black shawl that swung out and made the candles flicker.

"Mae gen i dipyn o dŷ bach twt
A'r gwynt i'r drws bob bore.

Hei di ho, di hei di hei di ho,
A'r gwynt i'r drws bob bore . . ."

sang the singers, and so sang Nain, in her high quivering voice.

The Lloyds thought it the funniest thing they had ever seen, and clutching their sides, they rolled on the floor, gasping and giggling.

Gwyn smiled, but he did not laugh. There was something strange, almost magical, about the tall figure spinning in the candlelight.

❋ ❋ ❋

Down in the field, Gwyn's father heard the music. For a few moments he paused and listened while his cows, eager to be milked, ambled on up to the farmyard. Mr. Griffiths regarded the mountain, rising dark and bare beside the house, and remembered his daughter.

❋ ❋ ❋

When the boys had no breath left for dancing or laughter, Mrs. Griffiths tucked the record player away in its corner, stood up, and removed her apron. Then she patted her hair, smoothed her dress, and said, rather quiet and coy, "The rest of the party will be in here today, boys!" and she walked across the hall and opened the door to the front room.

Gwyn was perplexed. Meals, even fairly proper meals with relatives, were always in the kitchen these days. He moved uncertainly toward the open door and looked in.

A white cloth had been laid on the long oak table, so white

it almost hurt his eyes. And upon the cloth was the best blue china, red napkins, and plates piled with brightly wrapped cookies, sugar mice, and chocolate pigs. There were chips and popcorn, and cakes with colored icing on a silver stand. There were noisemakers, too, decorated with gold and silver paper, and in the center of the table stood a magnificent green Jell-O mold, rising above a sea of ice cream.

The Lloyds crowded into the doorway beside Gwyn and gazed at the splendid spread. Gwyn felt so proud. "Oh, Mom," he said breathlessly. "Oh, Mom!" Then Gareth and Siôn rushed past him and drew out their chairs, exclaiming, "Gwyn! Gwyn, come on, let's start, we're starving!"

"It's the grandest birthday party I've ever seen," said Alun. "Our mom has never done anything like this."

"Nor has his, until today," said Nain. "It was about time."

Gwyn took his place at the head of the table and they began. There was so much chatter and laughter that no one heard Mr. Griffiths come in from milking and go upstairs. And Mrs. Griffiths, happy and gratified, did not notice her husband's boots beside the back door, nor his coat upon the hook, when she went into the kitchen to get the birthday cake.

The cake was huge and white, and looked like a castle with chocolate windows and silver banners and, on each of the nine towers, a flaming candle.

"Turn out the lights!" cried Gareth, and he sprang to the switch, plunging the party into cozy candlelight again.

"Blow out the candles, Gwyn, and wish!" commanded Siôn.

Gwyn drew a deep breath and then paused. "Let's cut the cake and leave the candles," he said. "They look so good. Let's leave them till they die."

The candles were still lit when Mr. Griffiths came down-stairs again. Noisemakers were banging, and no one heard feet on the tiled kitchen floor, tapping in unfamiliar shoes. When the door opened, the tiny flames glowed fiercely for a moment, and then died.

Except for a white shirt Mr. Griffiths was dressed entirely in black. He stared at the table in cold disbelief.

The shock of the electric light jolted the party out of its cheerfulness. The birthday table looked spoiled and untidy; someone had spilled orange juice on the white cloth.

"What's this? Celebrating, are we?" Mr. Griffiths's mouth was tight, his face white with displeasure.

Siôn was still wearing the spectacle mask and his brothers began to giggle. He did resemble Mr. Griffiths.

"It's Gwyn's birthday, Ivor," Mrs. Griffiths explained nervously. "You're just in time for . . ."

"I know what day it is." Her husband spoke the words slowly, through clenched teeth, as though the taste was bitter. "There are candles wasting in the kitchen, chairs on the floor, and look at this — mess!" He flung out his hand, indicating the table.

"Sit down, Ivor Griffiths, you miserable man," said Nain, "and celebrate your son's birthday!"

"Miserable am I?" Mr. Griffiths's big red hands were clasped tightly across his chest, one hand painfully rubbing and pressing at the other. "Miserable am I, because I remember my own daughter who is gone? My daughter who went on this day, four years ago?"

Suddenly Mrs. Griffiths stood up. "Enough! We've had enough, Ivor!" she protested. "We remember Bethan, too. We've mourned her going every year on this day for four years. But it's Gwyn's birthday, and we've had enough of mourning! Enough! Enough!" She was almost crying.

Gwyn turned his head away. He did not want to look at the bright colors on the table; he did not want to see his friends' faces. He knew that his birthday was over. His mother was talking, but he could not listen to the words. She was taking his friends away, he heard them shuffling into the kitchen, murmuring good-bye, but he could not move. His father was still standing by the table, sad and silent in his black suit.

"How could you do that, Ivor?" Nain reproached her son as the front door slammed.

"How could I? I have done nothing. It was that one!" And he looked at Gwyn. "She is gone because of him, my Bethan is."

It was said.

Gwyn felt almost relieved. He got up slowly and pushed his chair neatly back to the table; then, without looking at his father, he walked out to the kitchen.

His mother was standing by the sink, waving to the Lloyds through a narrow window. She swung around quickly when she heard her son. "I'm sorry, Gwyn," she said quietly. "So sorry." She came toward him and hugged him close. Her face was flushed and she had put on her apron again.

"It was a great party, Mom! Thanks!" said Gwyn. "The other boys liked it, too, I know they did."

"But I wanted your father to —"

"It doesn't matter, Mom," Gwyn interrupted quickly. "It was grand. I'll always remember it!"

He drew away from his mother and ran up to his room, where he sat on the edge of his bed, smiling at the memory of his party and the way it had been before his father had arrived. Gwyn knew his father could not help the bitterness that burst out of him every now and then, and he had acquired a habit of distancing himself from the ugly words. He thought hard about the good times, until the bad ceased to exist.

A tiny sound caused him to go to the window. There was a light in the garden, and a lantern swaying in the evening breeze.

Gwyn opened the window. "Who's there?" he called.

He was answered by a high, girlish laugh, and then his grandmother's voice: "Remember your gifts, Gwydion Gwyn. Remember Math, Lord of Gwynedd, remember Gwydion and Gilfaethwy!"

"Are you being funny, Nain?"

There was a long pause and then the reply, "It's not a game I'm playing, Gwydion Gwyn. Once in every seven generations the power returns, so they say. Your father never had it, nor did mine. Let's find out who you are!"

The gate clicked shut, and the lantern went swinging down the lane, while the words of an old song rose and fell on the freshening wind, and then receded, until the light and the voice faded altogether.

Before he shut the window, Gwyn looked up at the mountain and remembered his fifth birthday. It had been a fine day, like today, but in the middle of the night a storm had broken. The rain had come pouring down the mountainside in torrents, boulders and branches rumbling and groaning in its path. The Griffiths family had awakened, pulled the blankets closer to their heads, and fallen asleep again, except for Gwyn. His black sheep was still up on the mountain. He had nursed her as a motherless lamb, tucking her in Mom's old sweater, cozy by the fire, feeding her with a bottle five times a day, until she had grown into a fine ewe.

"Please get her! Please save her!" Gwyn had shaken his sister awake again.

Bethan had grumbled but because she was older and because she was kind, she had complied.

The last time Gwyn saw her she had been standing by the back door in her red raincoat, testing the big outdoor lantern. It was the night after Halloween, and the pumpkin was still on the windowsill, grimacing with its dark gaping mouth and sorrowful eyes. Bethan had become curiously excited, as though she was going to meet someone very special, not just a lonely black ewe. "Shut the door tight when I am gone," she had whispered, "or the wind will howl through the house and wake Mom and Dad!" Then, swinging the yellow scarf around her dark hair, she had walked out into the storm. She had never been afraid of anything.

Through the kitchen window, Gwyn had watched the light

of the big lantern flashing on the mountainside until it disappeared. Then he had fallen asleep on the rug beside the stove.

They never saw Bethan again, though they searched every inch of the mountain. They never found a trace of her perilous climb on that wild night, nor did they find the black ewe. The girl and the animal seemed to have vanished!

CHAPTER TWO

Arianwen

UNLIKE MOST NOVEMBERS, CALM DAYS SEEMED ENDLESS THAT autumn. Gwyn had to wait three weeks for a wind. It was the end of the month, and the first snow had fallen on the mountain.

During those three weeks he found he could not broach the subject of his ancestors, though he dwelt constantly on Nain's words. Since his birthday the atmosphere in the house had hardly been conducive to talking about it. His father was remote and silent. His mother was in such a state of anxiety that, whenever they were alone, he found he could only discuss the trivia of their days: the farm, the weather, and his school activities.

But every morning and every evening, Gwyn would open his drawer and take out the yellow scarf. He would stand by his window and run his hands lightly over the soft wool, all the time regarding the bare, snowcapped mountain, and he would think of Bethan.

Then, one Sunday, the wind came, so quietly at first that you hardly noticed it. By the time lunch had been consumed, however, twigs were flying, the barn door was banging, and the howling in the chimney was loud enough to drive the dog away from the stove.

Gwyn knew it was time.

"Who were my ancestors?" he asked his mother.

They were standing by the sink, he dutifully drying the dishes, his mother with her hands deep in the soapy water. "Ancestors," she said. "Well, no one special that I know of . . ."

"No one?" he probed.

"Not on my side, love. Your grandfather's a baker, you know that, and before that, well . . . I don't know. Nothing special."

"What about Nain?"

Gwyn's father, slouched in a chair by the stove, rustled his newspaper, but did not look up.

Gwyn screwed up his courage. "What about your ancestors, Dad?"

Mr. Griffiths peered, unsmiling, over his paper. "What about them?"

"Anyone special? Nain said there were magicians in the family . . . I think."

His father shook the newspaper violently. "Nain has some crazy ideas," he said. "I had enough of them when I was a boy."

"Made you try to bring a dead bird back to life, you said," his wife reminded him.

"How?" asked Gwyn.

"Chanting!" grunted Mr. Griffiths. It was obvious that, just as Nain had said, his father had not inherited whatever strange power it was that those long-ago magicians had possessed. Or if he had, he did not like the notion.

"The magicians are in the old legends," mused Mrs. Griffiths. "One of them made a ship out of seaweed, Gwydion I think it . . ."

"Seaweed?" Gwyn broke in.

"I think it was and . . ."

"Gwydion?" Gwyn absentmindedly pushed his wet dish-cloth into an open drawer. "That's my name."

"Watch what you're doing, Gwyn," his mother complained. "You haven't finished."

"Math, Lord of Gwynedd, Gwydion, and Gilfaethwy. And it was Gwydion who made the ship? Me . . . my name!"

"It's what you were christened. Nain wanted it, but" — Mrs. Griffiths glanced in her husband's direction — "your father never liked it, not when he remembered where it came from, so we called you Gwyn. Dad was pretty fed up with all of Nain's stories."

Mr. Griffiths dropped his newspaper. "Get on with your work, Gwyn," he ordered, "and stop flustering your mother."

"I'm not bothered, Love."

"Don't argue and don't defend the boy!"

They finished the dishes in silence. Then, with the wind and his ancestors filling his thoughts, Gwyn rushed upstairs and opened the drawer. But he did not remove the seaweed. The first thing he noticed was the brooch, lying on top of the scarf. He could not remember having replaced it in that way. Surely the scarf was the last thing he had returned to the drawer. . . .

The sunlight, slanting through his narrow window, fell directly onto the brooch, and the contorted shapes slowly assumed the form of a star and then a snowflake; next a group of petals changed into a creature with glittering eyes before becoming a twisted piece of metal again. Something or somebody wanted him to use the brooch!

Gwyn picked it up and thrust it into his pocket. Grabbing his coat from a chair, he rushed downstairs and out of the back door. He heard a voice as he raced across the yard, calling him to do a chore. "But the wind was too loud, wasn't it?" he shouted joyfully to the sky. "I never heard anything!"

He banged the yard gate to emphasize his words and began to run through the field. After a hundred yards the land began to rise; he kept to the sheep track for a while, then climbed a wall and jumped down into another field, this one steep and bare. He was among the sheep now, scattering them as he bounded over mounds and boulders. Stopping at the next wall, he took a deep breath. The mountain had begun in earnest. Now he had to either walk or climb — running was impossible.

A sense of urgency gripped him — an overwhelming feeling that today, perhaps within that very hour, something momentous would occur.

He stumbled on, now on a sheep track, now heaving himself over boulders. He had climbed the mountain often, sometimes with Alun, sometimes alone, but the first time had been with Bethan, one long-ago summer. It had seemed an impossible task then, when he was not even five years old, but she had willed him to the top, comforting and cajoling him with her gentle voice. "It's so beautiful when you get there, Gwyn. You can see the whole world — well, the whole of Wales, anyway, and the sea, and clouds below you. You won't fall, I won't let you!" She had been wearing the yellow scarf that day. Gwyn remembered how it had streamed out across his head, like a banner, when they reached the top.

It was not a high mountain, nor a dangerous one — some might even call it a hill. It was wide and grassy, a series of gentle slopes that rose, one after another, patterned with stone walls and windblown bushes. The plateau at the top was a lonely place, however. From there only the empty fields and surrounding mountains could be seen, and far out to the west the distant gray line of the sea. Gwyn took shelter beside the tallest rock, for the wind sweeping across the plateau threatened to roll him back from where he had come.

He must surely have found the place to offer his brooch. *Give them to the wind,* Nain had said. Bracing himself against the rock, Gwyn extended his upturned hand into the wind and uncurled his fingers.

The brooch was snatched away so fast that he never saw what became of it. He withdrew his hand and waited for the wind to answer, not knowing what the answer would be, but wanting it to bring him something that would change the way things were, to fill the emptiness in the house below.

But the wind did not reply. It howled around Gwyn's head and tore at his clothes; then slowly it died away, taking, somewhere within its swirling streams and currents, the precious brooch, and leaving nothing in return.

Then, from the west, came a silver-white cloud of snow, within minutes obscuring the sea, the surrounding mountains, and the fields below. And, as the snow began to encircle and embrace him, Gwyn found himself chanting, "Math, Lord of Gwynedd, Gwydion, and Gilfaethwy!" This he repeated, over and over again, not knowing whether he was calling to the living or the dead. And all the while, huge snowflakes drifted silently about him, melting as they touched him, so that he did not turn into the snowman that he might otherwise have become.

Gwyn stood motionless for what seemed like hours, enveloped in a soft, serene whiteness, waiting for an answer. Yet, had Nain promised him an answer? In the stillness he thought he heard a sound, very high and light, like icicles on glass.

His legs began to ache, his face grew numb with cold, and when night clouds darkened the sky, he began his descent, resentful and forlorn.

The lower slopes of the mountain were still green because the snow had not touched them, and it was difficult for Gwyn to believe he had been standing deep in snow just minutes earlier. Only from the last field could the summit be seen, but by the time Gwyn reached the field, the mountain was obscured by mist, and he could not tell if snow still lay above.

It was dark when he got home. Before opening the back door he stamped his boots. His absence from the farm all day would not be appreciated, he realized, and he did not wish to aggravate the situation with muddy boots. He raised his hand to brush his shoulders free of the dust he usually managed to collect, and his fingers encountered something icy cold.

Believing it to be a snowflake or even an icicle, Gwyn plucked it off his shoulder and moved closer to the kitchen window to examine what he had found. His mother had not yet drawn the curtains, and light streamed into the yard.

It was a snowflake — the most beautiful he had ever seen, for it was magnified into an exquisite and intricate pattern: a star glistening like crystal in the soft light. And then the most extraordinary thing happened. The star began to move and Gwyn stared, amazed, as it gradually assumed the shape of a tiny silver spider. Had the wind heard him after all? Was he a magician then?

"Gwyn, is that you out there? You'll get no dinner if you hang about any longer." His mother had spied him from the window.

Gwyn closed his fingers over the spider and tried to open the back door with his left hand. The door was jerked back violently, and his father pulled him into the kitchen.

"What are you doing out there? You're late! Can't you open a door now?" Mr. Griffiths had flecks of mud on his spectacles; Gwyn tried not to look at them.

"My hands are cold," he said.

"Dinner'll be cold, too," grumbled Mr. Griffiths. "Get your boots off and sit down. Where were you this afternoon? You were needed. That crazy rooster's escaped again. We won't have a Christmas dinner if he doesn't stay put."

With some difficulty, Gwyn managed to remove his boots with his left hand. "I'm just going upstairs," he said airily.

"Gwyn, what are you up to?" asked his mother. "Wash your hands and sit down."

"I've got to go upstairs," Gwyn insisted.

"But Gwyn . . ."

"Please, Mom!"

Mrs. Griffiths shrugged and turned back to the stove. Her husband had begun to chew his food and was not interested in Gwyn's hasty flight through the kitchen.

Tumbling into his bedroom, Gwyn scanned the place for something in which to hide his spider. He could think of nothing but the drawer. Placing the spider gently on the yellow scarf, he pushed the drawer back, leaving a tiny space for air, then fled downstairs.

He got an interrogation in the kitchen.

Mrs. Griffiths began it. "Why did you run off like that this afternoon?" she complained. "Didn't you hear me call?"

"No, it was windy," Gwyn replied cheerfully.

"Well, what was it you were doing all that time? I rang Mrs. Lloyd. You weren't there."

"No," said Gwyn, "I wasn't!"

"Not giving much away, are you?" Mr. Griffiths muttered from behind a mug of tea. "It's no use trying to get that rooster now that it's dark," he went on irritably. "We'll have to be up early in the morning."

"Won't have any trouble waking if he's out," Gwyn snickered.

"It would take more than a rooster to wake you some mornings." His mother laughed. At least she had recovered her good humor.

After tea, Mr. Griffiths vanished into his workshop. His workload of farm repairs seemed to increase rather than diminish, and Gwyn often wondered if it was his father's way of avoiding conversation.

He thought impatiently of the drawer in his room, while his mother chattered about Christmas and the rooster. Then, excusing himself with a quick hug, Gwyn left his mother to talk to the cat, and trying not to show an unnatural enthusiasm for bed, crossed the hallway and climbed the stairs slowly, but two at a time.

His bedroom door was open and there appeared to be a soft glow within. On entering the room, Gwyn froze. There were shadows on the wall: seven helmeted figures, motionless beside his bed. He turned fearfully to locate the source of light. It came from behind a row of toy spacemen standing on the chest of drawers. Gwyn breathed a sigh of relief and approached the spacemen.

The silver spider had climbed out of the drawer. It was glowing in the dark!

Gwyn brushed his toys aside and hesitantly held out his hand to the spider. It crawled into his open palm, and gently, he raised it closer to his face. The spider's touch was icy cold, and yet the glow that it shed on his face had a certain strange warmth that seemed to penetrate every part of his body.

He held the spider for several minutes, admiring the exquisite pattern on its back and wondering whether there was more to the tiny creature than a superficial beauty. It had come in exchange for the brooch, of that he was certain. But was it really he who had transformed the brooch? Or had the extraordinary spider come from a place beyond his world? He resolved to keep it a secret until he could consult his grandmother the following evening.

Replacing the spider in the drawer, Gwyn went downstairs to get a book. When he returned, the glow came from the bedpost, and deciding that he had no need of an electric light, he sat on the bed and read his book beside the spider. It was an exceptional sensation, reading by spiderlight.

❄ ❄ ❄

Nain was gardening by lamplight when Gwyn found her. She was wearing her sun hat and a bright purple cardigan. The sky was dark and frost had begun to sparkle on the ground.

"It's a little late for that, isn't it?" said Gwyn, approaching his grandmother by way of the gravel path.

"I like to poke a few things around," she replied, "just to let them know I've got my eye on them."

"There's not much growing, Nain," Gwyn remarked. "Not that you can see anything in this light."

"There's potatoes!" she said defiantly, and heaved a plant out of the ground, scattering earth all over Gwyn's white sneakers. Not satisfied with this, she shook the plant violently, and Gwyn sprang back, too late to save the bottoms of his new school pants.

"Oh, Nain!" he cried. "What did you do that for? I'll get in trouble!"

"Why didn't you put your boots on, silly boy?" she replied. "There's mud all down the lane."

"I came for a chat, didn't I? How was I to know I'd be attacked by a crazy woman?"

"Ha-ha! Who's crazy, Gwydion Gwyn?" Nain loved being teased. "Have you brought good news? Are you a magician, then?"

"Can we go inside, Nain?" Gwyn fingered the matchbox in his pocket. He did not want to confide under the stars, someone could be listening out there in the dark.

"Come on, then! We'll leave the plants to doze for a bit and have a cup of tea." Nain dropped her potatoes, shook out her purple cardigan, and stamped across the garden to open the back door.

The inside of her house was like a bright bowl. All the corners had been rounded off with cupboards and bookcases, and upon every item of furniture was heaped a jumble of books, bright clothes, and exotic plants. The fronds of shawls, trailing leaves, and garlands of beads festooned the furniture to such a degree that its identity could not easily be ascertained. The only source of light was an oil lamp, and as this was partially obscured by a tall fern, the whole place had a wild and mystical air about it.

Somewhere through the jumble a kettle lurked, and soon it was whistling merrily while Nain sang from behind a screen embroidered with butterflies, and a canary chattered in its cage.

Gwyn looked around for a vacant seat. There were none. "What shall I do with the eggs, Nain?" he called.

"How many?"

Gwyn counted the eggs, which were nestling in a red wooly hat on the only armchair. "Seven," he replied.

"Well, well! They've all been in here today and I never noticed." Nain chuckled to herself.

"Why d'you let the hens in, Nain?" Gwyn asked. "They're such dirty things. Mom would have a fit."

"Huh! Your mom would have a fit if she looked under my bed, I expect," Nain said, giggling, "but there's no need to go upsetting people for nothing. Bring the eggs out here."

Gwyn held out the bottom of his sweater and gathered the eggs into it. He looked for his grandmother behind the screen but she had vanished, and so had the kitchen. There was only a narrow space between rows of plants and yards of crimson velvet. He found the kettle on the windowsill and put the eggs in a green hat beside it. Nain did not seem to be short of hats, so he felt the eggs would be safe enough for the moment. However, she had been known to wear two at a time and so he called out, "Don't put your green hat on yet, Nain!"

His grandmother's head popped out from a gap in the velvet. "Isn't it grand?" she purred. "I'm going to dance in it."

"The hat?" Gwyn inquired.

"This, silly boy." His grandmother stroked the crimson material.

"Where?" he asked.

"Who knows?"

"Nain, would you find yourself a cup of tea and then sit down and concentrate? I've got something to show you!" Gwyn fingered his matchbox again.

"Was it the wind?" Nain asked. "It was windy yesterday. I thought of you. Quick, a cup of tea." She withdrew her head and reappeared a moment later, carrying two blue enamel mugs. "One for you?"

"No thanks, Nain!" His grandmother did not use conventional tea leaves. Her tea was made from nettles or dried roots.

Sometimes it was palatable, most often it was not. Today Gwyn preferred not to risk it.

He waited until his grandmother had settled herself in the armchair and sipped her tea before he knelt beside her and took out the matchbox. He wanted her undivided attention for his revelation. Even so he was unprepared for the ecstatic gasp that accompanied Nain's first glimpse of the spider, when he gently withdrew the lid. The tiny creature crawled onto his hand, glowing in the dark room, and Nain's eyes sparkled like a child's. "How did it come?" Her whisper was harsh with excitement.

"In the snow," Gwyn replied. "I thought it was a snowflake. It was the brooch, I think. I gave it to the wind, like you said, and this . . . came back!"

"So," Nain murmured triumphantly, "you are a magician then, Gwydion Gwyn, as I thought. See what you have made!"

"But did I make it, Nain? I believe it has come from somewhere else. Some far, far place . . . I don't know, beyond the world, I think."

"Then you called it, you brought it here, Gwydion Gwyn. Did you call?"

"I did, but . . ." Gwyn hesitated. "I called the names you said: Math, Lord of Gwynedd, Gwydion, and Gilfaethwy. Those were the only words."

"They were the right words, boy. You called to your ancestors. The magicians heard your voice and took the brooch to where it had to go, and now you have the spider!" Nain took the spider from Gwyn and placed it on her arm. Then she got up and began to dance through the shadowy wilderness of her room. The tiny glowing creature moved slowly up her purple sleeve, until it came to her shoulder, and there it rested, shining like a star beneath her wild black curls.

Gwyn watched and felt that it was Nain who was the magician and he the enchanted one.

Suddenly his grandmother swooped back, and taking the spider from her hair, put it gently into Gwyn's hands. "Arianwen," she said. "White silver! Call her Arianwen — she must have a name!"

"And what now?" asked Gwyn. "What becomes of Arianwen? Should I tell someone about her? Take her to a museum?"

"Never! Never! Never!" said Nain fiercely. "They wouldn't understand. She has come from another world to bring you closer to the thing you want."

"I want to see my sister," said Gwyn. "I want things the way they were before she left."

Nain looked at Gwyn through half closed eyes. "It's just the beginning, Gwydion Gwyn, you'll see. Recognize that you'll be alone. You cannot tell anyone. A magician can have his heart's desire if he truly wishes it, but he will always be alone." She propelled her grandson gently but firmly toward the door. "Go home now or they'll come looking, and never tell a soul!"

CHAPTER THREE
The Girl in the Web

THE FARMHOUSE WAS EMPTY WHEN GWYN REACHED HOME.
Mr. Griffiths could be heard drilling in his workshop. Mrs.
Griffiths had popped out to see a neighbor, leaving a note for
her son on the kitchen table:

SOUP'S ON THE STOVE
HEAT IT UP IF IT'S COLD

"The soup or the stove?" Gwyn muttered to himself. He opened
the stove door, but the red embers looked so warm and comforting he was reluctant to cover them with fresh coal. He
turned off the light and knelt beside the fire, holding out his
hands to the warmth.

He must have put the matchbox down somewhere and he
must have left it open, because he suddenly became aware that
Arianwen was climbing up the back of the armchair. When she
reached the top she swung down to the arm, leaving a silver
thread behind her. Up she went to the top again, and then
down, her silk glistening in the firelight. Now the spider was

swinging and spinning back and forth across the chair so fast that Gwyn could only see a spark, shooting over an ever-widening sheet of silver.

"A cobweb!" he breathed.

And yet it was not a cobweb. There was someone there. Someone was sitting where the cobweb should have been. A girl with long pale hair and smiling eyes: Bethan, sitting just as she used to sit, with her legs tucked under her, one hand resting on the arm of the chair, the other supporting her chin as she gazed into the fire. And still Arianwen spun, tracing the girl's face, her fingers and her hair, until every feature became so clear that Gwyn felt he could have touched the girl.

The tiny spider entwined the silk on one last corner and then ceased her feverish activity. She waited, just above the girl's head, allowing Gwyn to contemplate her creation without interruption.

Was the girl an illusion? An image on a silver screen? No, she was more than that. Gwyn could see the impression her elbow made on the arm of the chair, the fibers in her skirt, the lines on her slim, pale hand.

Only Bethan had ever sat like that. Only Bethan had gazed into the fire in such a way. But his sister was dark, her cheeks were rosy, and her skin was tanned golden by the wind. This girl was fragile and so silver-pale that she might have been made of gossamer.

"Bethan?" Gwyn whispered, and he stretched out his hand toward the girl.

A ripple spread across the shining image, as water moves

when a stone pierces the surface, but Gwyn did not notice a cool draft entering the kitchen as the door began to open.

"Bethan?" he said again.

The figure shivered violently as the door swung wider, and then the light went on. The girl in the cobweb hovered momentarily and gradually began to fragment and to fade until Gwyn was left staring into an empty chair. His hand dropped to his side.

"Gwyn! What are you doing, Love? What are you staring at?" His mother came around the chair and looked down at him, frowning anxiously.

Gwyn found that speech was not within his power, part of his strength seemed to have evaporated with the girl.

"Who were you talking to? Why were you sitting in the dark?" Concern caused Mrs. Griffiths to speak sharply.

Her son swallowed but failed to utter a sound. He stared up at her helplessly.

"Stop it, Gwyn! Stop looking at me like that! Get up! Say something!" His mother shook his shoulders and pulled him to his feet.

He stumbled over to the table and sat down, trying desperately to drag himself away from the image in the cobweb. The girl had smiled at him before she vanished, and he knew that she was real.

Mrs. Griffiths ignored him now, busying herself about the stove, shoveling in coal, warming up the soup. By the time the meal was ready and sat steaming in a bowl before him, he had recovered enough to say, "Thanks, Mom!"

"Perhaps you can tell me what you were doing, then?" his mother persisted, calmer now that she had done something practical.

"I was just cold, Mom. It's nice by the stove when the door is open. I sort of . . . dozed . . . couldn't wake up." Gwyn tried to explain away something his mother would neither believe nor understand.

"Well, you're a funny one. I would have been here but I wanted to pickle some of those tomatoes and I had to run down to Betty Lloyd's for sugar." Mrs. Griffiths chattered on, somewhat nervously Gwyn thought, while he sat passively, trying to make appropriate remarks in the few gaps that her commentary allowed.

His father's return from the workshop brought Gwyn to life. "Don't sit down, Dad!" he cried, leaping toward the armchair.

"What on earth? What's got into you, boy?" Mr. Griffiths was taken by surprise.

"It's a matchbox," Gwyn explained. "In the chair. I don't want it squashed."

"What's so special about a matchbox?"

"There's something in it, a particular sort of insect," stammered Gwyn. "For school," he added. "It's important, see?"

His father shook the cushions irritably. "Nothing there," he said and sat down heavily in the armchair.

"Here's a matchbox," said Mrs. Griffiths, "on the floor." She opened the box. "But there's nothing in it."

"Oh no!" Gwyn moaned.

"What sort of insect was it, Love? Perhaps we can find it for you." His mother was always eager to help where school was concerned.

"A spider," Gwyn said.

"Oh Gwyn," moaned Mrs. Griffiths, "not spiders. I've just cleaned this house from top to bottom. I can't abide cobwebs."

"Spiders eat flies," Gwyn retorted.

"There are no flies in this house," thundered Mr. Griffiths, "and when you've found your particular spider, you keep it in that box. If I find it anywhere near my dinner, I'll squash it with my fist, school or no school!"

"You're a mean old . . . man!" cried Gwyn.

Mrs. Griffiths gave an anguished sigh, and her husband stood up. But Gwyn fled before another word could be spoken. He climbed up to his bedroom and nothing followed, not even a shout.

He had turned on the light as soon as he entered the room, so he was not immediately aware of the glow coming from the open top drawer. He walked over to the window to draw the curtains and looked down to see Arianwen sitting on the whistle. Incredibly, she must have pulled the whistle from beneath the yellow scarf. But, on consideration, Gwyn realized it was a small feat for a creature who had just conjured a girl into her web. And what of the girl now? Had she been mere gossamer after all, a trick of the firelight on a silver cobweb?

"Why couldn't you stay where you were?" Gwyn inquired of the spider. "You caused me a little trouble just now!"

Arianwen moved slowly to the end of the whistle, and it occurred to Gwyn that she had selected it for some special purpose.

"Now?" he asked in a whisper.

Arianwen crawled off the whistle.

Gwyn picked it up and held it to his lips. It was cracked and only a thin sound came from it. He shrugged and opened the window. Arianwen climbed out of the drawer and swung herself onto his sleeve.

"But there's no wind," he said softly, and he held his arm up to the open window. "See, no wind at all."

The spider crawled onto the window frame and ran up to the top. When she reached the center she let herself drop on a shining thread until she hung just above Gwyn's head, a tiny lantern glowing against the black sky.

Gwyn had been wrong. There was a wind, for now the spider was swaying in the open window and he could feel a breath of ice-cold air on his face.

"Shall I say something?" he mused. "What shall I say?"

Then, without any hesitation he called, "Gwydion! Gwydion! I am Gwydion! I am Math and Gilfaethwy!"

Even as he said the words, the breeze became an icy blast, rattling the window and tugging at his hair. He stepped back, amazed by the sudden violence in the air.

Arianwen spun crazily on her silver thread and the wind swooped into the room, tearing the whistle from Gwyn's hand and whisking it out through the open window.

Now the sound of the wind was deafening, and terrifying, too, for where a moment before, the land had lain tranquil in the frosty silence, there was now an uproar: a moaning, groaning, and screaming in the trees that was almost unearthly. Sheep on the mountain cried out in alarm and ran for shelter, and down in the yard the dog began to howl as though his very soul was threatened. Gwyn heard his father step outside to calm the dog. "It's a peculiar kind of wind," Gwyn heard him say.

Something shot into the bedroom and dropped, with a crack, onto the bare floorboards. It was a pipe of some sort: slim and silver like a snake. Gwyn stared at it apprehensively, then he slowly bent and picked it up. It was silky smooth and had an almost living radiance about it, as though it had no need of human hands to shine and polish it. Tiny, delicate lines encircled it: a beautiful pattern of knots and spirals, shapes that he had seen on a gravestone somewhere, and framing the pictures in one of Nain's old books.

Almost fearfully, he put the pipe to his lips, but he did not play it. He felt that it had not come for that purpose. He sat on the bed and ran his fingers over the delicate pattern.

The window stopped rattling, and the wind dropped to a whisper. The land was quiet and still again. Arianwen left her post and ran into the drawer.

Gwyn laid the pipe on his bedside table and went to shut the window. He decided that he was too tired to speculate on the evening's events until he was lying down. He turned off the light, undressed, and got into bed.

But he had awakened something that would not sleep and now he was to be allowed no rest.

For a few moments Gwyn closed his eyes. When he opened them he saw that Arianwen had spun hundreds of tiny threads across the wall opposite his bed. They were so fine, so close, that they resembled a vast screen. Still she spun, swinging faster and faster across the wall, climbing, falling, and weaving, not one thread at a time but a multitude. Soon the entire wall was covered, but the spider was not satisfied. She began to thread her way along the wall beside Gwyn's bed; over the door, over the cupboard, until the furniture was entirely covered with her irresistible flow of silk.

Gwyn was not watching Arianwen now. Something was happening in the web before him. He had the sensation that he was being drawn into the web, deeper and deeper, faster and faster. He was plunging into black silent space. A myriad of tiny colored fragments burst and scattered in front of him, and then nothing for minutes that seemed like hours. Then the moving sensation began to slow until he felt that he was suspended in the air above an extraordinary scene.

A city was rising through clouds of iridescent snow. First a tower, tall and white, surmounted by a belfry of finely carved ice; within the belfry a gleaming silver bell. Beneath the tower there were buildings, all of them white, all of them round and beautiful, with shining domelike roofs and oval windows latticed with a delicate network of silver — like cobwebs.

Beyond the houses there lay a vast expanse of snow; surrounding the snow, there were mountains, brilliant under the sun, or was it the moon hanging there, a huge sphere glowing in the dark sky?

Until that moment the city had been silent but suddenly the bell in the white tower began to sway and then it rang, and Gwyn could hear it, clear and sweet over the snow. Children emerged from the houses; children with pale faces and silvery hair, chattering, laughing, and singing. They were in the snow-fields now, calling to one another in high melodious voices. Was this where the pale girl in the web had come from?

Suddenly another voice called. His mother was climbing the stairs. "Is that you, Gwyn? Are you awake? Was that a bell I heard?"

The white world shivered and began to fade until only the voices were left, singing softly in the dark.

The door handle rattled and Mrs. Griffiths came into the room. For a moment she stood in the doorway, silhouetted against the landing light. She was trying to tear something out of her hair. At length she turned on the light and gave a gasp. "Ugh! It's a cobweb," she exclaimed, "a filthy cobweb!" For her, the silky threads did not glitter, they appeared merely as a dusty nuisance. "Gwyn, how many spiders have you got up here?"

"Only one, Mom," he replied.

"I can hear singing. Have you got your radio on? It's so late."

"I haven't got the radio on, Mom."

"What is it then?"

"I don't know, Mom." Gwyn was now as bemused as his mother.

The sound seemed to be coming from beside him. But there was nothing there, only the pipe. The city, the children, and even the vast cobwebs were gone.

Gwyn picked up the pipe and put it to his ear. The voices were there, inside the pipe. He almost dropped it in his astonishment. So they had sent him a pipe to hear the things that he saw, maybe millions of miles away. The sound grew softer and was gone.

"Whatever's that? Where did you get it?" asked Mrs. Griffiths, approaching the bed.

Gwyn decided to keep the voices to himself. "It's a pipe, Mom. Nain gave it to me."

"Oh! That's all." She dismissed the pipe as though it was a trivial bit of metal. "Try and get some sleep now, Love, or you'll never get up for the bus." She bent and kissed him.

"I'll get up, Mom," Gwyn assured her.

His mother went to the door and turned out the light. "That singing must have come from the Lloyds. They're always late to bed," she muttered as she went downstairs. "It's the cold. Funny how sound travels when it's cold."

Gwyn slept deeply but woke soon after dawn and felt for the pipe under his pillow. He drew it out and listened. The pipe was silent. It did not even look as bright, as magical as it had in the night. Gwyn was not disappointed. A magician cannot always be at work.

He dressed and went downstairs before his parents were awake. He had eaten his breakfast and fed the chickens by the time his father came downstairs to put the kettle on the stove.

"What's got into you?" Mr. Griffiths inquired when Gwyn sprang through the kitchen door.

"Just woke up early. It's a beautiful day, Dad!" Gwyn said.

This statement received no reply, nor was one expected. The silences that sometimes yawned between father and son created an unbearable emptiness that neither seemed able to overcome. But they had become accustomed to the situation, and if they could not entirely avoid it, they accepted it as best they could. It was usually Gwyn who fled from his father's company, but on this occasion he was preoccupied, and it was his father who left to milk the cows.

A few moments later, Mrs. Griffiths shuffled down the stairs in torn slippers, still tying her apron strings. She was irritated to find herself the last one down. "Why didn't someone call me?" she complained.

"It's not late, Mom," Gwyn reassured her, "and I had my breakfast."

His mother began to bang and clatter about the kitchen nervously. Gwyn retreated from the noise and went into the garden.

The sun was up now; he could feel the warmth of it on his face. The last leaves had fallen during the wild wind of the night before, and had bedecked the garden with splashes of red and gold. A mist hung in the valley, even obscuring his grandmother's cottage, and Gwyn was glad that he lived in high country, where the air and the sky always seemed brighter.

At eight o'clock he began to walk down toward the main road. The school bus stopped at the end of the lane at twenty minutes past eight every morning, and did not wait for stragglers. It took Gwyn all of twenty minutes to reach the bus stop. For a half mile the route he took was little more than a steep trail, rutted by the giant wheels of his father's tractor and the hooves of sheep and cattle. He had to leap over puddles, mounds of mud, and fallen leaves. Only when he had passed his grandmother's cottage did his passage become easier. Here the trail leveled off a little. The bends were less sharp and something resembling a road began to emerge. By the time it reached the Lloyds' farmhouse, the road had become a respectable size, blacktopped and wide enough for two passing cars.

The Lloyd children had just erupted through their gate, all seven of them, arguing, chattering, and swinging their bags. Mrs. Lloyd stood behind the gate, while little Iolo clasped her skirt through the bars, weeping bitterly.

"Stop it, Iolo. Be a good boy. Nerys, take his hand," Mrs. Lloyd implored her oldest child.

"Mom! Mom! Mom!" wailed Iolo, kicking his sister away.

"Mom can't come. Don't be silly, Iolo! Alun, help Nerys. Hold his other hand."

Alun obeyed. Avoiding the vicious thrusts of his youngest brother's boots, he seized Iolo's hand and swung him off his feet. Then he began to run down the lane while the little boy still clung to his neck, shrieking like a demon. The other Lloyds, thinking this was great sport for the morning, followed close behind, whooping and yelling.

Gwyn envied the noise, the arguments, even the crying. He came upon a similar scene every morning and it never failed to make him feel separate and alone. Sometimes he would hang behind, just watching, reluctant to intrude.

Today, however, Gwyn had something to announce. Today he did not feel alone. Different, yes, but not awkward and excluded.

"Alun! Alun!" he shouted. "I've got news for you."

Alun swung around, lowering Iolo to the ground, and the other Lloyds looked up at Gwyn as he came flying down the lane.

"Go on," said Alun. "What news?"

"I'm a magician," cried Gwyn. "A magician." And he ran past them all, his arms outstretched triumphantly, his satchel banging on his back.

"A magician," scoffed Alun. "You're crazy, Gwyn Griffiths, that's what you are," and forgetting his duty, he left Iolo on the lane and began to chase Gwyn.

"Crazy! Crazy!" echoed Siôn and Gareth, following Alun's example.

"Crazy! Crazy!" cried Iolo excitedly, as he raced down the lane, away from Mom and his tears.

Soon there were four boys, tearing neck and neck down the lane, and one not far behind; all shouting, "Crazy! Crazy! Crazy!" except for Gwyn, and he was laughing too much to say anything.

But the three girls, Nerys, Nia, and Kate, always impressed by their dark neighbor, stood quite still and murmured, "A magician?"

CHAPTER FOUR

The Silver Ship

NAIN HAD WARNED HIM THAT HE WOULD BE ALONE, BUT Gwyn had not realized what that would mean. After all, he had felt himself to be alone since Bethan left, but there had always been Alun when he needed company on the mountain or in the woods, to share a book or a game, to lend a sympathetic ear.

And for Alun the need had been as great. Gwyn was the one with an empty house and a quiet space to think and play in. And Gwyn was the clever one — the one to help with homework. It was Gwyn who had taught Alun to read. On winter evenings the two boys were seldom apart. Gwyn had never envisioned a time without Alun's friendship, and perhaps if he had kept silent, that time would never have come. But it never occurred to Gwyn that Alun would find it impossible to believe him. He felt that he only had to find the right words in order to convince his friend, and on the homeward journey, that same afternoon, he once again brought up the subject of magicians.

Iolo always raced ahead when they got off the school bus. The older children, however, were not so keen to run uphill. They lingered on the road, Siôn and Gareth arguing, the girls collecting wildflowers or colored leaves. Alun and Gwyn always brought up the rear.

"Have you heard of Math, Lord of Gwynedd?" Gwyn began innocently.

"Of course, he's in the old Welsh stories. Dad talks about them," Alun replied.

"And Gwydion?"

"Yes, and how he made a ship from seaweed," Alun's interest had been aroused.

"I'd forgotten. Dad never talks about it. But Nain reminded me — she's got more books than I've seen anywhere, except in the library."

"Your Nain's a bit nutty isn't she?" Alun had always been a little suspicious of Gwyn's grandmother.

"No! She's not nutty! She knows a lot," Gwyn replied. "She knew about me — about my being a magician!"

"Now I know she's nutty. And you are, too," Alun said good-naturedly.

Gwyn stopped and stood quite still. His words came slow and quiet, not at all in the way he had intended. "I'm not nutty. Things happened last night. I think I made them happen. I wasn't dreaming. I saw my sister, or someone like my sister. Nain said Math and Gwydion were my ancestors . . . and that I have inherited —" He could not finish for his friend had begun to laugh.

"They're in stories. They're not real people. You can't be descended from a story."

"You don't know," Gwyn began to jabber desperately. "I can

make the wind come. I saw another planet last night, very close. It was white and the buildings were white, and there was a tower with a silver bell, there were children, and this is the most fantastic part, I could hear them in a pipe that came from —"

"You're crazy! You're lying!" Alun cried bitterly. "Why are you lying? No one can see planets that close, they're millions and millions and millions of miles away!" And he fled from Gwyn still crying, "Liar! Liar! Liar!"

"How do you know, Alun Lloyd?" Gwyn called relentlessly. "You don't know anything. You're ignorant! I know what I know. And I know what I've seen!"

He had gone too far. He realized that before Alun sprang through his gate and followed his brothers up the path to the house, slamming the door behind him, to emphasize his distaste for Gwyn's conversation.

Gwyn was alone on the lane with Nerys, Nia, and Kate. The three girls had lost interest in their flowers and were staring at Gwyn in dismay. He could not bring himself to speak to them, and so passed by in awkward silence.

A half mile farther on, he reached his grandmother's cottage, and knowing she was the only person in the world who would believe him, unceremoniously burst in upon her. He was astonished at what he saw.

Nain had sewn up the red velvet dress. She was wearing it, and was standing in the center of her room like some exotic bird, surrounded by her flowering plants and gaudy paraphernalia. She had something shining on her forehead, huge rings on her fingers, and around her waist, a wide bronze chain.

"Nain!" said Gwyn, amazed. "Where are you going?"

"I'm staying here," his grandmother replied. "This is my castle — I have to defend it."

She was talking in riddles again. Gwyn decided to come straight to the point. "Nain, I had something else from the wind last night: a silver pipe, and there were voices from far away in it."

"Ah," said Nain. "Even when men whispered, Math could hear them. He could hear voices beyond any mortal ear! The pipe is from him!"

"And something happened," Gwyn went on, "in Arianwen's web!"

As he spoke his grandmother began to move about her room, but Gwyn knew she was listening to his story, and when he mentioned the girl in the web, she hovered before a huge gilt-framed mirror at the back of the room and said softly, "Gwydion Gwyn, you will soon have your heart's desire!"

"My heart's desire?" said Gwyn. "I believe I am a magician but I am not strong yet. I don't know if these things are happening to me because I have the power, or if they would have happened to anyone."

"You've forgotten the legends, haven't you, poor boy?" said Nain. "I used to read them to you long ago, but your father stopped all that when Bethan left. He stopped all the fun, all the joy. But he couldn't stop you, could he? Because you are who you are! Now I'll read you something."

In spite of the multitude of books scattered about the room, his grandmother always knew exactly where to find the one she needed. From beneath a blue china dog supporting a lopsided lampshade, she withdrew a huge black book, its leather cover scarred with age.

"The legends," she purred, stroking the battered spine. It looked so awesome and so old that Gwyn half expected a cloud of bats to fly out when his grandmother opened it.

She furled the train of her velvet dress around her legs, settled herself on a pile of cushions, and beckoned to him.

Gwyn peered at the book over his grandmother's shoulder. "It's in old Welsh," he complained, "I can't understand it."

"Huh!" She sighed. "I forgot. Listen, I'll translate. 'At dawn, rose Gwydion, the magician, before the cock crowed, and he summoned to him his power and his magic, and he went to the sea and found seaweed, and he held it close and spoke to it, then he cast it out over the sea, and there appeared the most marvelous ship . . .'" She turned the next few pages hurriedly, anxious to find the words that would convey to Gwyn what she wanted. "Ah, here," she exclaimed. "Now you will understand. 'Then, Gwydion's son subdued the land and ruled over it prosperously, and thereafter he became Lord over Gwynedd!'" She closed the book triumphantly.

"Well?" said Gwyn. "I don't think I understand yet."

"He was our ancestor, that Lord of Gwynedd," said Nain, "and so, it follows, was Gwydion."

"But they're in a story, Nain." In spite of himself, Gwyn found he was repeating Alun's words. "They're not real people."

"Not real?" Nain rose tall and proud out of her chair. "They're our ancestors," she said, glaring at Gwyn, and she slammed the book down on others that were piled on a table beside her.

Gwyn winced as a cloud of dust flew into his face. A tiny vase tottered precariously beside the books, happily coming to rest before it reached the edge of the table.

"But how do you know, Nain?" he quietly persisted.

"How do I know? How do I know? Listen!" Nain settled back onto the cushions and drew Gwyn down beside her. "My great-great-grandmother told me. She was a hundred years old and I was ten, and I believed her. And now I'll tell you something I've never told anyone, not even your father. She was a magician, my great-great-grandmother. She gave me the seaweed and the brooch and the whistle. 'Keep it for you-know-who,' she said, and I did know who."

"And the broken horse?"

Nain frowned. "I am afraid of that horse," she said thoughtfully. "I tried to burn it once, but I couldn't. It was still there when the fire died, black and grinning at me. I believe it is a dreadful thing, and she thought so, too, my great-great-grandmother. She tied a label on it, '*Dim hon!* Not this!' for it must never be used, ever. It must be kept safe, and locked away — tight, tight, tight. It is old and evil."

"I'll keep it safe, Nain. But what about the scarf? Your great-great-grandmother didn't give you that, did she?"

"No, not the scarf. That was my idea. I found it on the mountain, the morning after Bethan disappeared, but I didn't tell a soul. What would have been the use? I kept it for you."

"Why for me?"

"Can't you guess? I knew you would need it."

"And are you a magician, too, Nain?" Gwyn ventured.

"No." Nain shook her head regretfully. "I haven't the power. I've tried, but it didn't come to me."

"And how do you know it has come to me?"

"Ah, I knew when you were born. It was All Hallows Day, don't forget, the beginning of the Celtic New Year. Such a bright dawn it was, all the birds in the world were singing. Like bells, wasn't it? Bells ringing in the air. Your father came flying down the lane. 'The baby's on the way, Mom,' he cried. He was so anxious, so excited. By the time we got back to the house you were nearly in this world. And when you came and I saw your eyes, so bright, I knew. And little Bethan knew, too, although she was only four. She was such a strange one, so knowing yet so wild, sometimes I thought she was hardly of this world. But how she loved you. And your dad was so proud. What a morning!"

"He doesn't even like me now," Gwyn murmured.

"No, and that's what we have to change, isn't it?" Nain said gently.

Gwyn buried his face in his hands. "Oh, I don't know! I don't know!" he cried. "How can a spider and a pipe help me? And what has another world to do with Bethan? I've just had a fight with my best friend. He wouldn't believe me."

"I warned you never to betray your secret," Nain scolded him. "Never abuse your power. You must be alone if you are to achieve your heart's desire."

"What's the use of magic if no one knows about it?" Gwyn exclaimed irritably. "And how do I get my heart's desire?"

"You know very well," Nain replied unhelpfully. "Think about the scarf. Think about using it. And now you'd better leave me, and eat the supper that is getting cold on your mother's table."

The room had become dark without their noticing it. The fire had almost died and the few remaining embers glowed like tiny jewels in the grate. Gwyn was unwilling to leave his grandmother; he wanted to talk on into the night. But Nain was not of the same mind, it seemed. She lit a lamp and began to pace about her room, moving books and ornaments in a disturbed and thoughtless manner, as though she was trying either to forget or to remember something.

Gwyn pulled himself up from the pile of cushions and moved to the door. "Good night, Nain!" he said.

The tall figure, all red and gold in the lamplight, did not even turn toward him. But when he reluctantly slipped out into the night, words came singing after him: "*Cysgwch yn dawel,* Gwydion Gwyn! Sleep quietly!"

❆ ❆ ❆

When he got home the table was bare.

"Did your grandmother give you a meal?" his mother inquired, guessing where he had been.

"No," said Gwyn. "I forgot to ask."

Mrs. Griffiths smiled. "What a strange one you are!" She gave him a plate of stew that had been kept warm on the stove.

Gwyn could not finish the meal and went upstairs early, muttering about homework.

He did not sleep quietly. It was a strange, wild night. The restless apple tree beneath his window disturbed him. He dreamed of Nain, tall for her ten years, in a red dress, her black curls tied with a scarlet ribbon. She was listening to her great-great-grandmother, an old woman, a magician with long gray hair and wrinkled hands clasped in her dark lap, where a piece of seaweed lay, all soft and shining, as though it was still moving in water, not stranded on the knees of an old, old woman.

Gwyn gasped. He sat up, stiff and terrified. He felt for the bedside light and turned it on.

Arianwen was sitting on the silver pipe. Gwyn lifted the pipe until it was close to his face. He stared at the spider and the pipe, willing them to work for him. But they did not respond. He laid them carefully on the bedside table, and got out of bed.

His black watch told him that it was four o'clock, not yet dawn. He dressed and opened his top drawer. It was time for the seaweed. Yet he took out Bethan's yellow scarf, and without knowing why, wrapped it slowly around his neck, pressing it to his face as he did so, and inhaling once again the musty sweet smell of roses. He closed his eyes, and for a moment, almost thought that he was close to an answer. But he had forgotten the question. It was something his grandmother had said, something about using the scarf. Try as he might to remember, he felt the answer and the question slipping away from him, until he was left with only the tangible things: the scarf and the dry dusty stick of seaweed.

Gwyn tucked the seaweed into the pocket of his coat and went downstairs, letting himself out the back door and into the yard.

There was a pale light in the sky but the birds were still at rest. The only sounds came from sheep moving on the hard mountain earth, and frosty hedgerows shivering in the cold air.

He did not ascend the mountain this time, but wandered northward through the lower slopes, seeking the breeze that came from the sea. Here the land was steep and barren. There were few sheep, no trees, and no farms. Gigantic rocks thrust their way through the earth and torrents of ice-cold water tumbled over the stones. Gwyn longed for the comfort of a wall to cling to. The wide, dark space of empty land and sky threatened to sweep him away and swallow him. One step missed, he thought, and he would slip into nowhere.

And then he smelled the sea. Moonlight became dawn and colors appeared on the mountain. He was approaching the gentler western slopes. He started to climb upward gradually, field by field, keeping close to the stone walls, so that the breeze that had now veered into a wailing northeast wind would not confuse his steps.

Gwyn had passed the fields and was standing in the center of a steep stretch of bracken when it happened: The thing in his pocket began to move and slide through his fingers, causing him to withdraw his hand and regard the soft purple fronds of what had, a few moments before, been a dried-up piece of seaweed. The transformation was unbelievable. Gwyn held the plant out before him, and the slippery petal-like shapes flapped in the wind like a hovering bird. And then it was gone — the wind blew it out of his hand and out to sea. And all the birds above and below him awoke and called out, and the gray sky was pierced with light. In that moment Gwyn knew what he had to do.

He took off the yellow scarf and flung it out to the sky, calling his sister's name again and again, over the wind, over the brightening land and the upturned faces of startled sheep.

Then, from the west where it was still dark, where the water was still black under the heavy clouds, there came a light, tiny at first, but growing as it fell toward the sea. It was a cool light, soft and silver, and as it came closer, Gwyn could make out the shape of a billowing sail and the bows of a great ship. But the ship was not in the sea. It was in the air above it, rising all the time, until it was opposite him and approaching the mountain.

A wave of ice-cold air suddenly hit Gwyn's body, throwing him back into the bracken, and as he lay there, shocked and staring upward, the huge hull of the silver ship passed right over him, and he could see fragments of ice, like sparks, falling away from it. He could see patterns of flowers and strange creatures engraved in the silver, and then the ice was in his eyes and he had to close them and curl himself into a ball, shaking with the pain of the bitter cold that enveloped him.

A dull thud shook the ground: Something scraped across the rocks and filled the air with a sigh.

Gwyn lay hidden in the bracken for a long time — cold, curled up tight, with eyes closed, too frightened and amazed to move. When he finally stood up, the cold, cold air was gone. He looked behind, around, and above himself, but the mountain was empty. There was snow on the bracken and in one flat field beyond the bracken, but no sign of a ship of any kind. Yet he had seen one, heard one, felt the bitter cold of its passage through the air.

Gwyn began to run. Now that it was light, he had no difficulty in finding his way across the northern slopes. Soon he was back in familiar fields, but when he came to within sight of Tŷ Bryn he paused a moment, then kept on running down the track, past his gate, past his grandmother's cottage, until he reached the Lloyds' farmhouse. He flung open the gate, rushed up the path, and ignoring the bell, beat on the door with his fists, shouting, "Alun! Alun! Come quick! I want to tell you something! Now! Now! Now!"

Within the house someone shouted angrily, it must have been Mr. Lloyd. Then footsteps could be heard, pattering on the stairs and approaching down the passage.

The front door opened and Mrs. Lloyd stood there, in a pink dressing gown, with rollers in her hair, her face all red and shiny.

"Whatever is it, Gwyn Griffiths?" she said. "Accident or fire?"

"No fire, Mrs. Lloyd. I want Alun. I have to tell him something. It's urgent!"

"No fire, no accident," snapped Mrs. Lloyd. "Then what are you doing here? We haven't even had breakfast. Why can't it wait till school?"

"Because it just happened!" Gwyn stamped his foot impatiently. "I've got to see Alun."

Mrs. Lloyd was angry. She was about to send Gwyn away, but something about the boy, standing tense and dark against the dawn clouds, made her hesitate. "Alun! You'd better come down," she called. "It's Gwyn Griffiths. I don't know what it's about, but you'd better come."

"Shut that door," Mr. Lloyd shouted from above. "I can feel the cold up here."

"Come inside and wait!" Mrs. Lloyd pulled Gwyn into the house and shut the door. "I don't know — you've got nerve these days, you boys."

She shuffled away into the kitchen, leaving Gwyn alone in the shadows by the door. It was cold in the Lloyds' house. The narrow hallway was crammed with bicycles and boots, and coats half hanging on hooks; it was carpeted with odd gloves, felt-tip pens, comics, and broken toys, and there were two pairs of muddy jeans hanging on the banisters.

Alun appeared at the top of the stairs, in pajamas that were too small. He was trying to reduce the drafty gap around his stomach with one hand, while rubbing his eyes with the other. "What is it?" he asked sleepily.

"Come down here," Gwyn whispered. "Come closer."

Alun trudged reluctantly down the stairs and approached Gwyn. "Go on, then," he said.

Gwyn took a breath. He tried to choose the right words, so that Alun would believe what he said. "I've been on the mountain. I couldn't sleep, so I went for a look at the sea . . ."

"In the dark?" Alun was impressed. "You're brave. I couldn't do that."

"There was a moon. It was quite bright really." Gwyn paused. "Anyway, while I was there I . . . I . . ."

"Go on!" Alun yawned and clutched his stomach, thinking of warm oatmeal.

"Well — you've got to believe me." Gwyn hesitated dramatically. "I saw a spaceship!" He waited for a response, but none came.

"What?" Alun said at last.

"I saw a ship — fall out of space — it came right over the sea — it was silver and had a sort of sail — and it was cold, so cold, I couldn't breathe from the cold of it. I had to lie down all curled up, it hurt so much. And when I got up — it had gone!"

Alun remained silent. He stared at his bare toes and scratched his head.

"Do you believe me? Tell me!" Gwyn demanded.

There was no reply.

"You don't believe me, do you?" Gwyn cried. "Why? Why? Why?"

"Sssssh! They'll hear!" Alun said.

"So what?"

"They think you're loony already."

"Do you? Do you think I'm loony?" Gwyn asked fiercely. "I did see a ship. Why don't you believe me?"

"I dunno. It sounds impossible — a sail and all. Sounds silly. Spaceships aren't like that."

Gwyn felt defeated. Somehow he had used the wrong words. He would never make Alun believe, not like this, standing in a cold hallway before breakfast. "Well, don't believe me then," he said, "but don't tell, either, will you? Don't tell anyone else."

"OK! OK!" said Alun. "You'd better go. Your mom'll be worried!"

"I'll go!" Gwyn opened the door and stepped down onto the porch, but before Alun could shut the door, he said again, "You won't tell what I said, will you? It's important!"

Alun was so relieved at having rid himself of Gwyn's disturbing presence, he did not notice the urgency in his friend's voice. "OK!" he said. "I've got to shut the door now, I'm freezing!"

He was to remember Gwyn's words — too late!

CHAPTER FIVE

Eirlys

ALUN DID TELL. HE DID NOT MEAN TO HURT OR RIDICULE Gwyn, and he only told one person. But that was enough.

The one person Alun told was Gary Pritchard. Gary Pritchard told his gang: Merfyn Jones, Dewi Davis, and Brian Roberts. Dewi Davis was the biggest gossip in the school and within two days everyone at Pendewi Primary had heard about Gwyn Griffiths and his spaceship.

Little whispering groups were formed in the playground. There were murmurings in the cafeteria, and children watched while Gwyn ate in silence, staring steadily at his plate of fries so that he should not meet their eyes. Girls giggled in the coatroom and even five-year-olds nudged one another when he passed.

And Gwyn made it easy for them all. He never denied that he had seen a silver ship, nor did he try to explain or defend his story. He withdrew. He went to school, did his work, sat alone on the playground, and spoke to no one. He came home, fed the hens, and ate his dinner. He tried to respond to his mother's probing chatter without giving too much away, for he felt he had to protect her. He did not want her to know that his friends thought he was crazy. Mrs. Griffiths sensed that something was wrong and was hurt and offended that her son did not confide in her; he had never shut her out before.

And then one evening, Alun came by. He had tried in vain to talk to Gwyn during their walks home from the bus, but since the gossiping began, Gwyn had taken pains to avoid his old friend. He had run all the way home, passing the Lloyds on the lane, so that he would not hear them if they laughed.

Mrs. Griffiths was pleased to see Alun. Perhaps he knew something. She let him into the kitchen saying, "Look who's here! We haven't seen you for a while, Alun. Take your coat off!"

"No!" Gwyn leaped up and pushed Alun back into the hall, slamming the kitchen door behind him. "What d'you want?" he asked suspiciously.

"Just to talk," Alun said nervously.

"What's there to talk about?"

"About the things you said, about the spaceship, and stuff," Alun replied, fingering the buttons on his coat.

"You didn't believe me, and you told," Gwyn said coldly.

"I know. I know and I'm sorry. I just wanted to talk about it." Alun sounded desperate.

"You want to spread more funny stories, I suppose?"

"No . . . no," Alun said. "I just wanted to —"

"You can shove off," said Gwyn. He opened the front door and pushed Alun out onto the porch. He caught a glimpse of Alun's white face under the porch light, and shut the door. "I'm busy," he called through the door, "so don't bother me again."

And he was busy, he and Arianwen. Every night she spun a web in the corner of Gwyn's attic bedroom, between the end of the sloping ceiling and the dresser, and there would always be something there in the web. A tiny, faraway landscape, white and shining, strange trees with icy leaves, a lake — or was it a sea? — with ice floes bobbing on the water, and a silver ship with sails like cobwebs, gliding over the surface.

And when he ran his fingers over the silver pipe, he could hear waves breaking on the shore; he could hear icicles singing when the wind blew through the trees, and children's voices calling over the snow. And he knew, beyond any shadow of a doubt, that he was hearing sounds from another world.

Once again, Arianwen spun a larger cobweb, covering an entire wall. The white tower appeared and the same houses. Children came out to play in the square beneath the tower. Pale children with wonderfully serene faces, not shouting as earthbound children would have done, but calling in soft, musical voices. It began to snow and suddenly they all stood still and turned to look in the same direction. They looked right into the web. They looked at Gwyn and they smiled, and then they waved. It was as though someone had said, "Look, children! He's watching you! Wave to him!" And their bright eyes were so inviting Gwyn felt a longing to be with them, to be touched and soothed by them.

But who had told the children to turn? Gwyn realized he had never seen an adult in the cobwebs, never heard an adult voice. Who was looking after the faraway children? Perhaps they had just seen the thing that was sending the pictures down to

Arianwen's web. A satellite, perhaps, or a ship, a star, or another spider, whirling around in space, and they had turned to wave to it.

❄ ❄ ❄

A few weeks before the end of term, three new children appeared at Pendewi Primary. They were children from the city, two boys from poor families who had no room for them, and a girl, who was an orphan. They had all been put into the care of Mr. and Mrs. Herbert, a warm-hearted couple with four girls, a large farmhouse, and an eagerness to foster children less fortunate than their own.

John, Eirlys, and Dafydd were officially entering the school the following term, but had been allowed three weeks of settling in before Christmas vacation. Miss Pugh, the principal, was a little put out. She had expected only two children, eight-year-old boys, to put in a class where there was still space for at least five more. There were thirty children in Gwyn's class, where Eirlys would have to go. Mr. James, their teacher, a fastidious man, was already complaining that he could feel the children breathing on him. He gave Eirlys a tiny desk at the back of the class, where no one seemed to notice her.

In the excitement of Christmas preparations, some of the children forgot about Gwyn and his stories. But for Gary Pritchard and his gang, teasing Gwyn was still more entertaining than anything else they could think of, especially when they saw a flicker of anger beginning to appear in their victim's dark eyes.

And then, one Monday, Dewi Davis went too far. It was a

bright, cold day. Snow had fallen in the night, clean white snow that was kicked and muddied by children running to school. But the snow fell again during the first lesson and as luck would have it, stopped just before the first recess, and the children were presented with a beautiful white playground in which to slide and throw snowballs.

Dewi Davis never could resist a snowball, just as he could never resist shoving girls with white socks into puddles, or putting worms down the backs of the squeamish. He took a lot of trouble with Gwyn's snowball; he patted and shaped it until it was rock hard and as big as his own head. Then he followed Gwyn around the playground, while the latter, deep in thought, made patterns in the snow with his feet.

Soon Dewi had an audience. Children drew back and watched expectantly while Gwyn trudged unaware through the snow. Dewi stopped about ten feet behind Gwyn, and called, in his slow lisping voice, "Hullo, Mr. Magic. Seen any spaceships lately?"

Gwyn began to turn, but before he could see Dewi, the huge snowball hit him on the side of the face and a pain seared through his ear and into his head.

Girls gasped and some giggled. Boys shouted and laughed, and someone said, "Go on, get him!"

Gwyn turned a full half-circle and stared at Dewi, stared at his fat silly face and the grin on his thick pink lips, and he wanted to hurt him. He brought up his clenched right fist and thrust it out toward Dewi, opening his fingers wide as he did so, and a low hiss came from within him, hardly belonging to him, and not his voice at all, but more like a wild animal.

There was nothing in Gwyn's hand, no stone, no snow, but something came out of his hand and hit Dewi in the middle of his face. He saw Dewi's nose grow and darken to purple, and saw anguish and amazement on Dewi's fat face. Only he and Dewi knew that there had been nothing in his hand.

Then, suddenly, the rest of the gang were upon Gwyn. Someone hit him in the face, someone punched his stomach, his hair was tugged, his arms jerked backward until he screamed, and then his legs were pulled out from under him, and he crashed onto the ground.

Everyone stopped shouting: They stared at Gwyn, motionless in the mud and snow. And then the bell rang, and almost simultaneously, Dewi began to scream for attention. The children drifted away while Mr. James ran to Dewi and helped him from the playground. He never noticed Gwyn lying in the corner.

The whole of Gwyn's body ached, but his head hurt most of all. He could not get up and did not want to. There was blood on the snow beside him, and his lip felt swollen and sticky. The playground was empty, and he wondered if he would have to lie there all day. Perhaps the snow would fall again and no one would see him until it was time to go home. He managed to pull himself up until he was kneeling on all fours, but it was quite an effort and he could not get any farther because something in his back hurt whenever he moved.

And then he saw that he was not alone. Someone was standing on the other side of the playground. Someone in gray with long, fair hair and a blue hat. It was Eirlys. The girl began to walk toward Gwyn. She walked slowly, as though she was approaching a creature she did not wish to alarm. When she reached Gwyn, she bent down and put her arms beneath his and around his body. Then, without a word, she began to lift him to his feet. She looked very frail, and Gwyn could not understand where her strength came from. Her hair, beneath his hands, was so soft it was like touching water, and her face, now close to his, was almost as pale as the snow. He had never really looked at her before and realized with a shock that he knew her. He had seen her somewhere but could not remember where.

They walked across the playground together, still without speaking, his arm resting on her shoulders, her arm around his waist, and although his legs ached, he tried not to stumble or lean too heavily on the girl. When they reached the school door, Eirlys withdrew her arm and then took his hand from her shoulder. Her fingers were ice-cold, and Gwyn gasped when she touched his hand.

"What is it?" she asked.

"You're so cold," Gwyn replied.

Eirlys smiled. Her eyes were greeny-blue, like arctic water; it was as though they had once been another color, but that other color had been washed away.

When they got to the classroom, Gwyn told Mr. James that he had slipped in the snow. Eirlys said nothing. Mr. James nodded. "Get on with your work now," he said.

Eirlys and Gwyn went to their desks. Everyone stared. Dewi Davis was still holding his nose, and Gwyn remembered what he had done. All through the next lesson, through the pain in his head, he kept thinking of what he had done to Dewi. He had hit him with magic. Something had come out of his hand and flown into Dewi's face, something that had come to him from Gwydion, the magician, and from Gwydion's son, who had once ruled Gwynedd. And it was the same thing that had turned the seaweed into a ship, the brooch into a spider, and the whistle into a silver pipe. These last three, he realized, had merely been waiting for him to release them: They had been there all the time, just waiting for his call. But when he had hit Dewi, he had done it by himself. He had wanted to hurt Dewi, wanted to smash his silly, cruel face, and he had done it, not with a stone or with his fist but with his will and the power that had come from Gwydion. If he could do that, what could he not do?

While Gwyn dreamed at his desk, he was unaware that Eirlys was watching him. But Alun Lloyd noticed, and he wondered why the girl gazed at Gwyn with her aquamarine eyes. He was uneasy about the things that were happening.

During the day, Gwyn's aches and pains faded and he was able to hobble to the school bus unaided. When he got off the bus, however, he could not run up the lane as he had been doing, and he felt trapped because Alun was lingering behind the rest of his family, watching him.

"You OK?" Alun asked Gwyn.

"Yes, I'm OK."

"D'you want me to walk up with you?"

"No," Gwyn replied. "I said I was all right, didn't I?"

"Are you sure?" Alun persisted. He turned to face Gwyn and began to walk up the hill backward.

"They didn't hurt me that bad," Gwyn said angrily. "I just can't walk that fast."

"I suppose she's going to help you?" Alun said. He was still walking backward and looking at someone behind Gwyn.

"Who?"

"Her!" Alun nodded in the direction of the main road and then turned and ran up the lane.

Gwyn glanced over his shoulder to see what Alun had meant. Eirlys was walking toward him.

"What are you doing?" Gwyn shouted. "You don't get off here."

The girl just smiled and kept coming.

"You'll be in trouble! How're you going to get home?"

"I'll walk," said Eirlys.

"Oh no!" cried Gwyn.

"Don't worry!" The girl continued her approach, and Gwyn waited, unable to turn his back on her.

"It'll be all right," the girl said when she was beside him. "I'll just come home with you. You might need someone, with all those bruises." She tapped his arm and began to precede him up the hill.

When they turned a bend and Nain's cottage suddenly came into view, Eirlys stopped and stared at the building.

"My grandmother lives there," Gwyn said.

"Does she?" Eirlys spoke the words not as a question, but as a response that was expected of her.

She passed the cottage slowly, trailing her fingers along the top of the stone wall, so that sprays of snow flew out onto her sleeve, but she never took her eyes off the light in Nain's down-stairs window.

Gwyn was tempted to take the girl in to see his grandmother, but it was getting dark and they still had to pass the furrows of snow that had drifted into the narrow track farther on. He wondered how on earth Eirlys was going to get home. "What will Mrs. . . . What's-her-name say, when you're not on the bus?" he asked.

"Mrs. Herbert? She's kind. She'll understand," Eirlys replied.

They held hands when they reached the snowdrifts, Gwyn leading the girl to higher ground at the edge of the trail. Once again he gasped at the icy touch of her fingers, and when Eirlys laughed the sound was familiar to him.

She was reluctant to come into the farmhouse, and when Gwyn insisted, she approached it cautiously with a puzzled frown on her face, and every now and then she would look away from the house and up to where the mountain should have been, but where, now, only a moving white mist could be seen.

"Come on," said Gwyn. "Mom'll give you a cup of tea."

He opened the front door and called into the kitchen, "I'm back, Mom. Sorry I'm late. I had a little bit of trouble with the snow."

"I thought you would," came the reply.

His mother was stirring something on the stove when he went into the kitchen. She turned to speak to him but instead cried out, "Your face! What happened?"

"I had a fight. It's not anything, really!" Gwyn said.

His father got up from the chair by the kitchen table, where he had been mending some electrical equipment; he was about to be angry, but then he saw Eirlys standing in the doorway. "Who's this?" he asked.

"Eirlys!" said Gwyn. "She helped me. She walked up from the bus with me, to make sure that I was all right."

"That was kind of you, Eirlys," said Mrs. Griffiths. "Take your coat off and warm up. I'll make a pot of tea."

She began to help Gwyn with his coat, exclaiming all the time at the state of his muddy clothes and the bruises on his face.

Eirlys came into the room and took off her hat and coat. She drew a chair up to the table and sat down opposite Mr. Griffiths. He just stood there, staring at her, while his big hands groped for the tiny brass screws that had escaped him and now spun out across the table.

The girl caught one of the screws and stretched across to put it safely into his hand. Gwyn heard the sharp intake of breath as his father felt the girl's icy fingers, and he laughed. "She's cold-blooded, isn't she, Dad?" he said.

Mr. Griffiths did not reply. He sat down and began his work again. Mrs. Griffiths poured the tea and brought a fruitcake out of the pantry. They discussed the snow and the school and the fight. Mrs. Griffiths asked how and why the fight had begun, and although Gwyn could not give a satisfactory explanation, Mr. Griffiths did not say a word, he did not even seem to be listening to them, but every now and then he would look up and stare at Eirlys.

When it was dark, Mrs. Griffiths expressed concern for the girl. "You'd better phone your mom. She'll be worried," she said.

"She hasn't got a mom," Gwyn answered for the girl. "She's living with the Herberts."

"Oh, you poor love." Mrs. Griffiths shook her head sympathetically.

"They're lovely," said Eirlys brightly. "So kind. They won't mind. They'll come and get me. They said they would if I wanted, and it's not far."

"No need for that." Mr. Griffiths suddenly stood up. "I'll take you in the Land Rover."

Gwyn was amazed. His father never usually offered lifts. "You're being honored," he whispered to Eirlys as Mr. Griffiths strode out the back door.

By the time Eirlys had gathered up her hat and coat and her schoolbag, the deep throbbing of the Land Rover's engine could be heard out in the lane.

"Good-bye," said Eirlys. She walked up to Mrs. Griffiths and kissed her. Mrs. Griffiths was startled; she looked as though she had seen a ghost.

She remained in the kitchen while Gwyn and the girl walked down to the gate. The door of the Land Rover was open and Mr. Griffiths was standing beside it. "You'll have to get in this side and climb over," he told Eirlys. "The snow's deep on the other side."

Gwyn had never known his father to be so considerate to a child.

Eirlys stepped out into the lane, but before she could climb into the Land Rover, Mr. Griffiths's arms were around her, helping her up. For a second the two shadowy figures became one and, for some reason, Gwyn felt that he did not belong to the scene. He looked away to where the frozen hedgerows glittered in the glare of the headlights.

Inside the house, the telephone began to ring. Then the Land Rover's wheels spun into movement, and Gwyn had to back away from the spray of wet snow. It was too late to shout good-bye.

He turned to go back into the house and saw his mother standing on the porch. "Mrs. Davis was on the phone," she said gravely. "She wants to talk to us tomorrow. It's about Dewi's nose!"

CHAPTER SIX

A Drowning

"WE'VE LEFT DEWI WITH HIS AUNTIE," SAID MRS. DAVIS.

Dewi had many aunties. Gwyn wondered which one had the pleasure of his company, and if Dewi was to be envied or pitied.

The Davises had come to "thrash out the problem of the nose," as Mr. Davis put it.

It was six o'clock. The tea had only just been cleared away, and Gwyn's stomach was already grumbling. They were sitting around the kitchen table: Mr. and Mrs. Davis, Gwyn, and his parents — as though they were about to embark on an evening of cards or some other lighthearted entertainment, not something as serious as Dewi's nose.

"The problem, as I see it," began Mrs. Davis, "is, who's lying?"

"Gary Pritchard, Merfyn Jones, and Brian Roberts all say that they think they saw Gwyn throw a stone," said Mr. Davis solemnly. "Now, this is very serious business."

"Very dangerous, too," added Mrs. Davis.

"That goes without saying, Gladys," Mr. Davis coughed.

"Now, the situation is . . ." He paused dramatically. "What's to be done about it?"

"How . . . er, how bad is his nose?" Mrs. Griffiths asked.

"Very bad," replied Mrs. Davis indignantly. "How bad do you think your nose would be if it had been hit by a rock?"

"Now wait a minute!" Mr. Griffiths entered the conversation with a roar. "First it's a stone, now it's a rock, and we haven't yet established whether anything was thrown. Perhaps Dewi bumped his nose. We haven't heard his explanation."

"That's the problem." Mr. Davis banged his fist on the table. "Dewi says he did bump his nose, but the other boys say Gwyn hit him with a stone."

"Dewi's frightened of him!" Mrs. Davis pointed an accusing finger at Gwyn. "He's afraid your boy'll do something worse to him if he tells."

"Nonsense!" Mr. Griffiths stood up, his chair scraping on the tiled floor. "Let's hear your side of it, Gwyn."

Gwyn looked up. He was not used to having his father defend him. He felt that he could take on any number of Davises now. "I didn't throw a stone," he said.

"There!" Mr. and Mrs. Griffiths spoke simultaneously.

Mr. Griffiths sat down and the two sets of parents eyed each other wordlessly.

"He's lying, of course," Mr. Davis said at last.

"He ought to be punished," added his wife. "The principal should be told."

"It's a pity they don't spank kids these days," growled Mr. Davis.

This time it was Mr. Griffiths who banged on the table. Gwyn got up and began to pace around the room while the adults all talked at once. He had a tremendous desire to do something dramatic and the knowledge that he probably could made the temptation almost unbearable. What should he do, though? Box Mr. Davis's ears from a distance of ten feet? Pull Mrs. Davis's hair? The possibilities were endless. And then he remembered Nain's warning. He must not abuse his power. It must be used only when there was something that he truly needed to do.

"It's not as if your son is normal," he heard Mrs. Davis say. "Everyone's been talking about his being peculiar, if you know what I mean. Ask any of the children."

For the first time, his parents seemed unable to reply. Mrs. Griffiths looked so miserable that Gwyn could hardly bear it. She had known for days that something was wrong, and now she was going to hear about his stories.

"It seems," Mrs. Davis went on, "that Gwyn has been saying some very peculiar things, if you know what I mean. And why? If you ask me your son's not normal."

Gwyn had to stop her. Contemplating the generous curves that overflowed the narrow kitchen chair supporting Mrs. Davis, his eyes alighted upon a large expanse of flesh, just above the knee, that her too-tight skirt could not cover. He flexed his fingers, then pressed his thumb and forefinger together — tight, tight, tight!

Mrs. Davis screamed. She glared at Mr. Griffiths and then asked haughtily, "Have you got a dog?"

The two men frowned at her and then frowned at each other, while Mrs. Griffiths said, "Yes, he's in the barn!"

"A cat?" Mrs. Davis inquired hopefully.

"A black tom." Mrs. Griffiths nodded toward a dark form sitting on the sill, outside the kitchen window. "We call him Long John," she went on, "because he lost a leg on the road when he was just a kitten. It's wonderful what vets can do these days."

Mrs. Davis glanced at Long John then quickly looked away, her cyclamen-pink lips contorted with distaste. "I think we'll go," she said and stood up.

Her husband looked at her but did not move.

"Get up, Bryn!" Mrs. Davis commanded. "I want to go!"

Mr. Davis followed his wife out of the kitchen with a bemused expression on his face. He could not understand why the interview had ended so abruptly, and wondered if the situation had been resolved without his being aware of it.

The Griffithses were as perplexed as he was. They silently followed their unwelcome guests to the front door, and there the whole unpleasant business might have ended, had not Mrs. Davis been heard to mutter darkly, "Someone pinched my thigh!"

Mrs. Griffiths gasped, and her husband roared, "What?" But Mr. Davis, having opened the front door, thrust his wife through it before she could cause the affair to deteriorate further. He then leaped quickly after her, and the wind parted the two families by slamming the door.

Mr. and Mrs. Griffiths retreated into the kitchen and slumped, battle-weary, beside the table. And then the humor of the situation overcame them and they began to laugh with relief.

"Thanks for sticking up for me, Dad," said Gwyn, when his parents had recovered. He felt awkward and not at all sure that he had done the right thing in the end.

"If you say you're innocent, that's all I need to know," said Mr. Griffiths gruffly.

Gwyn looked hard at his father; he could not understand his change of attitude. A week ago he would have been neither believed nor defended. In all probability he would have been sentenced to a weekend in his room and a meal of bread and water. "I'd better go do my homework," he said shyly.

He was about to leave the room when his father suddenly said, "Is that girl coming again?"

"What girl?" Gwyn asked.

"You know what girl. The one who was here yesterday. I can always run her home if" — his father hesitated and then added shyly — "if she wants to come."

"I don't think she will," said Gwyn. "She's a girl. She only came because I was hurt."

"Oh, was that it?"

Gwyn thought he could detect something almost like regret in his father's voice. What had come over his dad? It was quite disturbing. It had nothing to do with him, Gwyn was sure of that. He knew instinctively that he could not, should not, use his power to influence thought. The pinch had been satisfactory, though.

He remembered that his father's mood had changed when

Eirlys appeared. If that was the case, then she must come again, if only to keep his father happy. And so, although it was against his principles to have girls at Tŷ Bryn, the following day he asked Eirlys if she could come to the farm on Saturday.

"Of course," Eirlys replied, and her eyes shone with pleasure.

"Mom and Dad want it," said Gwyn, by way of explanation, "and . . . and so do I, of course!"

The weather changed. December brought sun instead of snow. The wind was warm and smelled of damp leaves and overripe apples.

Gwyn took Eirlys on his mountain, and she saw it in sunshine where before she had only glimpsed it at dusk, through a mist of snow. She saw the colors that he loved, the buzzards hunting low over the fields, and rosy clouds drifting above the plateau. He had not realized that he would enjoy the company of a girl. But then Eirlys was not like other girls.

They leaped — and sometimes slipped — on wet stones in the tumbling streams. They ran, arms outstretched, beside the stone walls, scattering the sheep that dozed there, and they chased crows that hopped, like black thieves, behind the leafless trees. And somehow Gwyn's father always seemed to be there, watching them from a distance, or walking nearby with his dog and his blackthorn stick, listening to their voices. And after tea he began to whistle in his workshop, and Gwyn realized he did not recognize the sound. Even his mother looked up, astonished, from her ironing.

In the evening, while it was still light enough to see the trees, the children walked in the orchard, and Gwyn told Eirlys about Nain and the five gifts; about the power that had come to him from Gwydion and how he had hit Dewi Davis without a stone. He told her about the silver ship that had caused all his trouble at school, and unlike Alun, Eirlys believed him and did not think it strange that a ship had fallen out of the sky. Even so, Gwyn did not speak of the snow spider. He was still wary of confiding too much. "I'll take you to see my grandmother," he told the girl. Nain would know whether he could tell Eirlys about the cobwebs.

Later, he asked his parents if Eirlys could come again, so that they could visit Nain.

"Why can't she stay the night?" Mr. Griffiths suggested. "She can sleep in Bethan's room."

"No!" cried Mrs. Griffiths, and then more quietly, "It's . . . it's just that the room isn't ready!"

Nothing more was said just then, but when Mr. Griffiths returned from his journey to the Herberts', he suddenly said, "Shall we ask the girl for Christmas? She can stay a day or two, and there'll be time to get the room ready."

"No!" his wife said again. "No! It's my Bethan's room."

"But she isn't here, Mom," Gwyn said gently.

"It's waiting for her, isn't it?" his mother reproached him.

"But Eirlys could sleep there," Gwyn persisted. "The room is ready — I looked in. The bed is made, and the patchwork quilt is on it. The dressers are shiny and all the dolls are there — it's such a waste!"

"Yes, all the dolls are there!" cried Mrs. Griffiths. She sank into a chair and bent her head, covering her face with her hands.

"You don't seem to care, anymore, either of you. It's my daughter's room, my Bethan's — her bed, her dolls, her place."

Her husband and her son stood watching her, sad and helpless. How could they tell her that it didn't matter if Bethan was not with them, because now there was Eirlys.

"We won't discuss it now," said Mr. Griffiths. "But I've already agreed to fetch the girl tomorrow. Be kind while she's here. She's an orphan, remember?"

"I won't upset her," Mrs. Griffiths said. "I'm sorry for her, she's just not my Bethan."

❄ ❄ ❄

When Gwyn took Eirlys to visit his grandmother the following afternoon, Nain was waiting by the gate. She had dressed carefully, in an emerald green dress and scarlet stockings for the occasion; around her neck she wore a rope of grass-green beads, long enough to touch the silver buckle on her belt, and from each ear a tiny golden cage swung, with a silver bird tinkling inside it.

Eirlys was most impressed. "How beautiful you look," she said, and won Nain's heart.

Gwyn noticed that his grandmother could not take her eyes off the girl. She watched her every move hungrily, like a bright-eyed cat might watch a bird. "Eirlys!" she murmured. "That's Welsh for 'snowdrop.' So we have a snowflower among us!"

After they had sipped their flowery tea and eaten cake that tasted of cinnamon and rosemary, Gwyn told his grandmother about the ship and Dewi Davis's nose, while Eirlys wandered around the room, touching the china, the beads, and the plants;

studying pictures in the dusty books, and tying colored scarves around her head.

Nain was not surprised to hear about the silver ship. She merely nodded and said, "Ah, yes!" But now that her prophecies for Gwyn were coming true, she found it almost too gratifying to bear. "You have nearly reached what you wanted, Gwydion Gwyn," she said. "But be careful! Don't do anything foolish!"

"Shall I tell Eirlys about the spider?" Gwyn asked his grandmother. "Should she know about the cobwebs and that other world?"

"Of course," said Nain. "Though I believe she knows already."

They left the cottage before dark. Nain followed them to the gate and as they set off up the track she called again, "Be careful!"

Gwyn was not listening to his grandmother; he had begun to tell Eirlys about the spider. He realized that he had not seen Arianwen for several days and wondered where she was.

When they got back to the farmhouse, Mrs. Griffiths was upstairs, sewing the hem on her new bedroom curtains. Her husband was cleaning the Land Rover. He had used it to transport a new flock of chickens from the Lloyds that morning, and they had made more of a mess than he had bargained for.

Gwyn told Eirlys to wait in the kitchen while he fetched the pipe and the spider from his attic room. When he returned, she was sitting in the armchair by the stove. The light was fading, but a tiny slither of winter sun had crept through the swaying branches of the apple tree and into the kitchen window. The light glimmered on the girl in the armchair, and Gwyn had to stop and take a breath before he said, "You are the girl in the web, Eirlys!"

"Am I?" she said.

"Yes, it was you! I knew it all the time, but I couldn't see how . . . You're like my sister, too. Where did you come from, Eirlys?"

The girl just smiled her inscrutable smile and asked, "Where is the spider?"

"I don't know," he replied. "I looked in the drawer, on top of the dresser, and under the bed. I couldn't find her."

Eirlys looked concerned. "Where can she be?" she asked.

Gwyn shrugged. "I don't know. She's been gone before, but only for a day. I haven't seen her for nearly a week."

His father called through the front door, "Time to go, Eirlys. Are you ready?"

Eirlys stood up. "You must find the spider, Gwyn," she said. "She's precious! She will make it possible for you to see whatever you want, and when I . . ."

"When you what?" Gwyn demanded.

"I can't say just yet," Eirlys replied. And then she disappeared into the hall and ran out of the house before Gwyn had time to think of another question.

He watched the lights of the Land Rover flickering on the lane before he climbed up to his room again. This time he shook the curtains, felt under the carpet, and beginning to panic, emptied the contents of every drawer upon the floor. Arianwen was not there.

He went down to the kitchen to see his mother. "Have you seen that spider?" he inquired.

"I've seen too many spiders," Mrs. Griffiths replied. She was rolling pastry on the kitchen table and did not look up when she spoke.

"But have you seen my own particular spider?"

"I saw one, yes. It could have been the one." Mrs. Griffiths inexorably rolled and rolled the pastry and did not look up. "It was different," she went on, "a sort of gray."

"Silver!" Gwyn corrected her. "Where was it?"

"Here. On the curtain."

"Did you catch it?"

"Yes! You know I can't abide cobwebs." Mrs. Griffiths had finished the pastry, but still she did not look up.

"What did you do with it?"

"I put it down the drain," his mother said flatly. "Drowned it!"

Gwyn was speechless. He could not believe what he had heard. His mother had to be joking. He stared at her, hoping for a smile and a teasing word, but she kept tearing little pieces away from the pastry and would not look at him.

And then Gwyn found himself screaming, "Drowned? Drowned? You can't have!"

"Well, I did!" At last his mother faced him. "You know I don't like spiders. Why did you keep it so long?" She could not explain to Gwyn that she was afraid not only of the spider but of the strange girl who could not be her daughter, yet seemed so like her, and who was beginning to take her daughter's place.

"You don't understand!" Gwyn cried. "You foolish woman. You don't know what you've done!" He ran to the kitchen sink. "Did you put it down here? Where does the drain go to?"

"The septic tank," Mrs. Griffiths said defiantly. Guilt was making her angry. "And you can't look there. Nothing can live in that stuff. The spider's dead."

CHAPTER SEVEN
The Broken Horse

"NO! NO! NO!" GWYN RUSHED OUT OF THE KITCHEN AND UP to his room. He regarded the dark places where cobwebs had sparkled with snow from that other world. The room seemed unbearably empty without them. He flung himself onto the bed and tried to tell himself that Arianwen was not gone forever. Surely he had the power to bring her back?

But he had nothing left for the wind. All Nain's gifts had been used up: the brooch, the whistle, the seaweed, and the scarf. Only one thing remained — the broken horse.

Gwyn got up and went over to the chest of drawers. He tried to open the top drawer but it appeared to be stuck. He shook it, and the silver pipe rolled off the top. He bent to pick it up, and as he touched it, a sound came from it, like whispering or the sea.

He ignored the sound and left the pipe on his bed while he continued to wrestle with the drawer. It suddenly burst open and almost fell out from the force that Gwyn had exerted on it.

The black horse lay within — it was alone and broken, grotesque without ears and a tail. Its lips were parted as if in pain, and Gwyn was overwhelmed by a feeling of pity. He took the horse out of the drawer and examined it closely. "*'Dim hon!'*" he murmured, reading again the tiny scrap of yellowed paper tied to its neck. "'Not this!' Why 'Not this'? This is all I have!"

From the bed the pipe whispered, "Not this! Not this! Not this!"

But Gwyn was not listening.

❋ ❋ ❋

The following morning, Gwyn woke up with a sore throat and a cold.

"You'd better stay indoors," his mother told him over breakfast. "No use getting worse or spreading your germs."

Gwyn was about to remark that other people carried germs, too, but thought better of it. He would not mind missing a day of school and if, by some miracle, Arianwen should have escaped the septic tank, she would fare better if she had a friend nearby.

"I'm not staying in bed!" he said sulkily. He had not forgiven his mother.

"I didn't say in bed," she retorted.

"I don't want to stay indoors, either."

"Please yourself! I'm only thinking of your health!"

Mr. Griffiths did not seem to be aware of the acrimony flying around the breakfast table. He took himself off to the milking shed, still whistling.

Gwyn went up to the attic and put on his coat. The sun was shining and the air was warm. He went downstairs and out through the back door into the yard. To the left of the yard, a row of barns formed a right angle with a long cowshed directly opposite the back door. To the right, a stone wall completed the enclosure. Within the wall a wide gate led on to the mountain track, and somewhere in the field beyond that gate lay the septic tank.

Gwyn wandered toward the gate, climbed over it, and jumped down into the field.

A circle of hawthorn trees surrounded the area where the septic tank lay, buried under several feet of earth. The trees were ancient, their gray branches scarred with deep fissures. It always came as a surprise when white blossoms appeared on them in spring. Sheep had ambled around the thorn trees and nibbled the grass smooth. Not even a thistle had been left to give shelter to a small stray creature.

Gwyn stood at the edge of the circle and contemplated the place where Arianwen may have ended her journey from the kitchen sink. He imagined her silver body whirling in a tide of black greasy water, and he was filled with helpless rage.

Thrusting his hands deep into his pockets, he stepped away from the hawthorn circle and began to stroll up the mountain. As the track wound upward, the field beside it sloped gently down toward the valley until, a mile beyond the farmhouse on a sharp curve, there was a sheer drop of thirty feet between the track and the field below. Here Gwyn stopped, where a low stone wall gave some protection for the unwary. There was something hard in his right pocket; he withdrew his hand and found that he was holding the broken horse. He must have slipped it into his pocket by accident the night before.

He stared at the poor broken thing, and then looked back at the farmhouse. A wreath of smoke streamed from the chimney into the blue sky. A blackbird sang in the orchard, and he could see his mother hanging out the laundry. A breeze had set the pillowcases flying, and a pink curtain flapped from an upstairs window. It was such a peaceful, ordinary scene. And then his gaze fell on the ring of thorn trees, and he hated the morning for being beautiful while Arianwen was dying in the dark.

Gwyn swung out his right hand and hesitated. The horse seemed to be staring at him with its wild lidless eyes, inviting him to set it free — its maimed mouth was grinning in anticipation. All at once, Gwyn felt afraid of what he was about to do, but his grasp had slackened, and in that moment, a gust of wind tore the horse away and his hand tightened on empty air. The wind carried the tiny object over a flock of sheep that neither saw nor cared about it, but some of the animals raised their heads when the boy above them cried out, "Go! Go then, and bring her back to me if you can! Arianwen! Arianwen! Arianwen!"

The broken horse vanished from sight, and as it did so, a low moan rumbled through the air. A black cloud passed across the sun and the white sheep became gray.

Gwyn turned away to continue his walk, but after he had taken a few paces it began to rain, only a few drops at first, but then suddenly it was as if a cloud had burst above and water poured down upon his head in torrents. He began to run back down the track and by the time he reached the house, the rain had become a hailstorm. His mother was bundling the wet laundry back into the kitchen, and he took an armful from her, fearing that it was he who had brought the storm upon them.

And what a storm it was. Sudden, frightening, and ferocious.

It beat upon the windows and tore into the barn roofs, causing the cattle to shift and grumble in their stalls. It shook the gates until they opened and terrified sheep poured into the garden and the yard. The hens shrieked and flapped their battered, soaking wings as they ran to the henhouse. And once there they did not stop their noise but added their voices to the terrible discord of the other animals.

The sky turned inky black and Mrs. Griffiths put the lights on in the house, but the power failed and they were left in the dark, surrounded by the sounds of distressed creatures that they could not help.

Mr. Griffiths burst through the back door, his big boots shiny with mud.

"The road's like a river," he exclaimed. "I've never seen anything like it."

"What is it, Ivor?" whispered his wife. "It was such a beautiful day."

"Just a storm." Mr. Griffiths tried to sound calm. "It'll blow itself out eventually."

Will it? Gwyn thought. *Have I done this?*

They lit a candle and sat around the table drinking tea. Mrs. Griffiths seemed to be the only one capable of speech. "Whatever's happened?" she kept murmuring. "It's like the end of the world. And Gwyn with a cold, too."

The storm abated a little in the afternoon. The hail turned to rain again, and they were able to attend to the animals. But the air still cracked and rumbled, and the dog was too terrified to work effectively. Gwyn and his father had a hard time driving the sheep out of the garden and through torrents of running mud, to the field.

They managed to get the ewes into an open barn, where they remained, anxious but subdued.

"They'll lose their lambs if it goes on like this," said Mr. Griffiths.

The yard had become a whirlpool, and they had to use a lantern to find their way safely to the cowsheds. The cows were in a state of panic. They trembled and twisted, bellowing mournfully. In the light of the lantern, the whites of their eyes bulged in their black faces, and though they were full of milk, they refused to be touched.

Mr. Griffiths loved his black cows. He loved to be close to them and he still milked by hand, ignoring the cold electrical apparatuses other farmers preferred. He stood in the cowshed suffering with his animals, dismayed by their condition.

"What is it?" he muttered. "It can't be the storm. I've never seen them like this."

"Leave them till later, Dad," Gwyn suggested. "They'll calm down when the wind dies."

"It's like the devil's in there," said his father, closing the big door on his cattle.

They waded back to the kitchen door, leaving their wet raincoats and boots on the narrow porch outside. A stream of water followed them into the room, but for once, Mrs. Griffiths did not seem concerned. She was looking out of the window on the opposite side of the room. "I'm thinking about Nain," she said. "The lane is like a river, her front door rattles even in a breeze, and you never fixed her roof in spring like you said you would, Ivor."

"I'll go and see her in a bit." Her husband sighed and sank into a chair.

"I'll go," Gwyn offered. He wondered how Alun and the other Lloyds had fared in the storm.

❋ ❋ ❋

The Lloyds were already at home. Fearing that her little ones would be soaked if they had to walk up the lane, Mrs. Lloyd had picked up her family by car. And just as well, for Iolo was shaking with fear. He hated thunder.

Alun was in the room he shared with his brothers. He was standing by the window, watching the rain while the twins argued on the floor behind him. Alun enjoyed a storm — he relished the noise and the violence. He gazed at the contortions of the trees, hoping that one might fall. And then he saw something.

Someone was out in the storm. Someone small and alone: a pale shape, moving slowly against the wind and the water.

The figure stopped opposite the Lloyds' gate, on the other side of the lane. Alun saw a face, white in the light from the window, looking up at him, and he knew who it was. Her hood had fallen back and her soaking hair hung in ash-colored strands over her hunched shoulders. She was holding one arm across her chest and looked frightened and exhausted.

Alun quickly drew the curtains and turned away from the window.

"What is it?" asked Gareth. "What did you see out there? You look funny."

"I didn't see anything," Alun replied. "Only the storm."

"Looks like you saw a ghost to me," said Siôn.

✣ ✣ ✣

Gwyn was on the front porch, pulling on his boots. His mother helped him with his raincoat, buttoning it tightly at the neck.

"Don't be long, now," she said. "Just pop in and see if your grandmother needs anything. Come straight back or your cold'll get worse."

"It's gone," said Gwyn. "The water washed it away." He tried to laugh, but the sound stuck in his throat.

He ran down the side of the track where the ground was higher, leaping from island to island, his lantern beaming on the lane ahead to ensure that the rivulets of mud had not encroached upon the remaining patches of dry land.

When he reached his grandmother's cottage, the rain suddenly stopped, and beneath the clouds, an eerie yellow light crept across the horizon. The dripping trees stood black against the sky, and the only sounds came from innumerable streams gushing down the mountainside.

There was no light in Nain's cottage. Gwyn knocked but there was no reply. He opened the door and looked in. His grandmother's room was cold and dark. There was something dreadfully wrong about the place, an oppressive stillness that frightened him. He turned on the light and saw what it was.

Beneath a gray veil of ashes, Nain's treasures lay in ruins. Pictures hung at crazy angles around the room, and once-bright scarves drooped in colorless shreds. The canary lay motionless at the bottom of its cage, and all across the floor were fragments of glass, books ripped and spoiled, shattered beads, and dying plants.

Some terrible element had crushed and abused everything in the room that was a part of his grandmother. Every object that she had chosen, nurtured, and loved had been destroyed.

Beside the dead fire from where the flying ashes had scattered, Nain sat huddled in a chair. She seemed older, smaller than before. There were ashes in her black hair and her face was gray.

Gwyn stepped slowly over the broken possessions until he stood beside his grandmother. "What happened, Nain?" he asked. "What has been here?"

Nain looked up at him and her black eyes narrowed. "You know very well, Gwydion Gwyn," she said. "You know and I know what you have done. You bad, bad magician!"

"What have I done, Nain?" Even as he asked the question, Gwyn knew what the answer would be.

"You let it go! My great-great-grandmother trusted me, and I trusted you. You have failed us, Gwydion Gwyn!"

"You mean the broken horse, don't you?" Gwyn cried defiantly. "Well, say so then! Speak its name! It was all I had. Arianwen has gone, drowned perhaps, and I had to get her back. Eirlys said I must!"

"But why the horse? Why the horse?" Nain rose out of her chair and her voice rose with her. "Didn't I tell you to keep it safe? Never to let it go? The spider would have returned to you. A creature like that could never die. She belongs to you, and you can get her when you want to, if you really try."

"I didn't know how," said Gwyn. "And I didn't mean to let

the horse go. The wind took it. What is it, anyway, that I have released? And how can I stop it?"

"Only you can find that out, Gwydion Gwyn," his grand-mother replied. "And I am afraid for you. It is a strong and dreadful thing that you must capture!"

"But didn't you see it? It was here. Why did it do this to your room?"

"Ah!" Nain sank back into her chair. "I tried to stop it, see. When I heard that noise in the air and all the birds stopped singing, when the hail began to batter the land and the trees trembled, then I knew what you had done. So I went to my great-great-grandmother's books and I tried to find out how to stop it." Her voice sank to a whisper. "I burned leaves in a bowl, and some bones and berries, and I began to sing. But it knew, didn't it? It knew what I was doing and it came in through the door and knocked me down. It smashed my bowl and blew out the fire. It was so angry. It roared around the room and broke everything in its way, and then it left!"

"And didn't you see anything?"

"Nothing! It was in the wind!"

Gwyn was silent. He was terrified of the thing that he had to face, but determined to make things right. "I'll help you clean up, Nain," he said.

"Leave it to me!" she snapped. "They'll be needing you at home."

But Gwyn refused to go until he had helped his grandmother to sweep the debris from the floor. They gathered the dying plants and put them in water, dusted the furniture, and straightened the pictures. Gwyn picked up the torn pages and replaced them in the books, before his grandmother tenderly arranged them into piles again. He sifted out the broken china, and Nain put it in order, ready for gluing. After a while the room began to come to life again. But the canary still lay quiet at the bottom of its cage, its neck bent and its eyes closed.

"It could do this?" Gwyn asked, staring at the broken bird.

"It could do worse," Nain replied. "Go on now! And take this." From beneath the cushion on which she had been sitting, she withdrew the black book. "I kept one thing safe, you see," she said. "I knew you would need it."

It was dark when he left the cottage. The water was not so deep, and the thunder had rolled away, but there was a strange turbulence in the air that disturbed him.

He was relieved to see that the lights had come on again in the farmhouse. It looked safe and welcoming. His father met him at the door. "Did you see the girl?" he asked.

Before Gwyn could reply, his mother said, "Why were you gone so long? What happened?"

"I had to help Nain," he explained, and would have said more if his father had not interrupted again.

"Did you see the girl?" he demanded anxiously.

"The girl? Eirlys? No, I didn't see her," Gwyn said.

"Where is she?" His father sprang past him and strode across the lawn to where the Land Rover waited in its shed.

"The Herberts called," he shouted. "They said she left two hours ago. Slipped out of the house into the storm. Came to see if you were all right, they thought, because you weren't at school!"

He disappeared into the shed and the Land Rover burst into life. It crashed down onto the road and rocked and roared its way through the mud.

Two hours? Gwyn thought. *And in the storm. Did she fall somewhere and I didn't see?*

In the kitchen, his mother had laid four soup bowls on the table. "Your dad'll find her," she said, when she saw Gwyn's worried frown.

Gwyn was not so sure. There was that thing in the air. That awful something that had destroyed Nain's room.

They heard the Land Rover returning only minutes later, and Gwyn ran to open the front door. His father was already beside the vehicle. The door was swinging wide and he was gathering something into his arms: something gray that was streaked with mud.

Mr. Griffiths walked through the gate and up the garden path, and as he came within the arc of light thrown out by the porch light, they saw the gray bundle. The girl's pale hair was black with mud, her white face covered with smudges of brown, and she had lost her shoes.

Gwyn held his breath. He realized that he had known the girl for a long, long time. What a dumb magician he was, indeed, not to have understood, just because her hair was pale and her face white.

"I found her in the lane," said Mr. Griffiths, "just beside the Lloyds' wall. I don't know how they didn't see her. She's unconscious, the cold probably, but I can't find any broken bones."

"I'll ring Dr. Vaughan." Mrs. Griffiths ran to the telephone in the kitchen.

"She's staying here, Glenys," her husband called after her. "In Bethan's room. I'm not having them take her from us."

He carried the girl upstairs, and Gwyn followed, mopping at the drips with a paper towel. When Mrs. Griffiths had finished on the telephone, she ran up and covered the pillow with a towel, then they gently removed the wet gray coat and laid Eirlys on the bed.

They stood around the bed, and without saying a word, without even looking at one another, they knew that they had all seen the girl lying on the bright quilt. They had seen her there before, long ago. They knew that Bethan had come back.

"You go and have your tea. I'll stay with her." Mr. Griffiths moved a chair over to the bed.

Gwyn did not move.

"Don't worry, lad," his father said. "It's all over now."

Gwyn knew that it was not. He could not eat. He took the lantern down to the gate to watch for the doctor's car, and saw something black lying there, beside the hedge, all huddled in the mud.

Gwyn bent down and picked up poor Long John's limp body. The black cat's eyes were closed, his nose was full of earth. His three good legs had let him down at last, and he had drowned, unable to escape the malice of the storm.

"Who do you think you are, you THING?" Gwyn screamed into the night. "I'll get you! Just you wait!"

CHAPTER EIGHT
The Trap

THE DOCTOR CAME LATE. HE HAD MANY VISITS TO MAKE THAT night. Other mysterious accidents had occurred: falls, burns, and near-drownings.

When he had finished listening through his stethoscope, he held the girl's wrist for a long time, feeling her pulse. Something puzzled him. She reminded him of someone he had seen in the same house, in that very room, only the other had been dark with golden skin. "It seems you have recovered," said Dr. Vaughan. "But you had better stay where you are for a day or two."

"Watch her!" the doctor told Mrs. Griffiths before he went. "She's well, but her pulse is so weak I can hardly feel it. It's almost as though — no one was there."

Gwyn was allowed into the girl's room the following morning. It was still dark and the bedside light was on. She was sitting up, wearing one of Bethan's old nightgowns. Her hair had been washed and looked paler than ever.

It's strange how she hasn't grown, thought Gwyn. *Now we are the same size.*

She was gazing around at all the things that made the room

peculiarly Bethan's place: a group of rag dolls in faded cotton dresses on the dressing table, a picture of bluebells on the wall, a yellow dress in a plastic cover, still hanging on the back of the door, and the blue-and-pink forget-me-not curtains that Bethan had chosen.

They did not refer to the past, just then. They talked about the thing that had come hurtling out of the storm to throw her down into the mud, the terror of the animals, Nain's devastated room, and poor Long John.

"And it's my fault," said Gwyn. "I know it is. I gave something to the wind that I should not have given. An old, old broken horse. I was told to keep it safe, never to let it go, but I did. I wanted Arianwen back and I thought it was the only way."

"It seems to me," she said, "that if you are to stop the thing, you have to get its name, discover what it is."

"How can I do that?" Gwyn asked. "It could be one of a million names, like Rumpelstiltskin, and we can't wait that long. Who knows what damage it may do while we're searching for a name?"

She rested her chin upon her hand, like Bethan used to do, and said slowly, "If you are your namesake, if you are Gwydion, the magician from a legend, perhaps the broken horse is from a legend, too. Perhaps a demon from a true story was trapped inside the broken horse by magic, to keep its evil locked up, safe, away from the world."

Gwyn frowned. It seemed to make sense. It had felt so very old, that broken horse.

All at once the girl leaned forward and said quietly, "There was another gift, wasn't there? Nain gave you five; you have only told me about four of them!"

Gwyn looked hard at the girl in Bethan's bed, and then he said, "A yellow scarf. Your scarf, to bring you back!"

They grinned at each other, and Gwyn felt as though all the heavy air that he'd been holding tight inside himself was flowing out of him and he could breathe again. He had so many questions to ask and did not know which to choose. "Where have you been, Bethan?" he said at last.

"I'm not Bethan," she replied. "I might have been Bethan once, but now I'm Eirlys. I'll never be Bethan again. I've been out there!" She inclined her head, indicating a sliver of darkness dividing the forget-me-not curtains.

"On the mountain?"

"No." She seemed reluctant to continue and then said, "Out there! Farther than the mountain! Farther than the sky!"

"How?"

"It will be hard for you to believe."

"Go on. I know what it's like when people don't believe you. Tell me about the night you went to find the black ewe."

It was several minutes before Eirlys spoke again. Gwyn waited patiently while she searched for words to tell him what few people would believe.

"I wasn't frightened," she said slowly. "It was exciting out there with the rain shining in the light of the lantern. I had a feeling that something was going to happen. Something that I'd always wanted, but never understood. I couldn't find the black ewe. I called and called. You gave her a name, remember?

Berry! Because her wool was purply-black, like dark fruit. I had to go higher and higher, and it began to get cold. I'd forgotten my gloves and my fingers felt so stiff I could hardly hold the lantern. I wanted to rest and warm my hands in my pockets but I couldn't because of the lantern. And then I saw Berry. She was standing by that big rock, just past the last field, where it's quite flat, except for the rock. I called to her and I put out my hands — and I dropped the lantern. It was so black. I tried to move in the dark, but I fell. I rolled and rolled, I don't know how far, then I managed to grab a tuft of grass and stop myself."

The girl stopped speaking and stroked the patchwork quilt, spreading her fingers out, as though she wanted to feel her way back to a place where she had once belonged.

"I thought I was going to die," she went on, dreamily, "either from cold or falling or the wet. And then I saw a light, far away. There weren't any stars. The light came close and all around it the storm shone like a rainbow. I saw a sail and dancing creatures on a silver ship, just like you did. And I wanted to touch it, I wanted, so much, to be with it. . . ."

"And then?" Gwyn begged.

"They took me in!"

"Who took you in?"

"The children. Only they're not really children — they're very old, and very wise. But they have never grown — like me. They took me to that other world. The place you saw in the web!"

"And Berry?"

"Berry was there, too. She knew her name but her fleece was

silvery-gray instead of black. And my hair was pale and so was my skin. And I never grew, nor did she."

"Is it a good place?"

"Yes, it is."

"Why did you come back?"

"You called me, didn't you? At first your calls were very faint, and then when Nain gave you the gifts, your voice became so loud we couldn't ignore it. We sent the spider because you wanted to see me. She was all we had. That's how I could see you back here — in cobwebs!"

"Cobwebs?" said Gwyn. "You mean there are more spiders? And you use them like . . . like television?"

Eirlys looked pityingly at him. "Not like television," she said. "Our cobwebs are far more wonderful than that."

"Tell me more about the place out there. Could I go there?"

This time Eirlys ignored his question. "Find Arianwen!" she said.

"But how? Mom drowned her. She's out there, under the ground. I've nothing left, no gifts to get her back. And I don't know the words."

Eirlys stared at him. "You're a magician," she said. "You're Gwydion Gwyn. You can get her back. Try!"

Gwyn felt ashamed. Under the compelling gaze of those arctic eyes, he left the chair beside the bed and slipped silently out of the room.

He went downstairs and pulled on his boots. The rain had stopped and there was nothing to remind him that he would need a coat. He opened the front door and closed it noiselessly behind him. Within seconds he was standing outside the circle of hawthorn trees. There was something heavy in the air, forcing the gray, twisted branches to bend toward the earth, discouraging any passage beneath them.

Gwyn hesitated. Was it possible that even the trees were possessed? He stepped quickly into the circle and gasped as a thorn tore into his shoulder.

The wet ground was beginning to freeze and a white mist hung low over the grass. There was someone or something else within the circle. He could feel it drawing him back toward the thorn trees. In order to resist it he had to fling himself to the ground and crawl toward the center.

Once there, Gwyn did not know what to do. He tried to remember how he had felt when he had hit Dewi Davis, but this was different. Something was distracting him, tugging his mind away from what he wanted to do. He laid his head on the freezing earth and listened, but all he could hear was the air above him, crackling like angry fireworks. And then he, too, began to get angry. A deep hatred of the thing that had killed Long John boiled up inside him. He pushed and pushed against it with his mind until he felt it falling away, and he had a clear space in his head. He closed his eyes and thought of the bricks beneath the earth, the water from the kitchen sink within the bricks, the spider in the water. He brought up his hands to rest beside his head, thrust downward, and felt himself plunging through the earth — down, down, down!

❄ ❄ ❄

Mrs. Griffiths had come into the bedroom with a glass of milk. She gave the drink to Eirlys and then walked over to the window. "It's snowing again," she said. "What a start to the winter."

"I love the snow," said Eirlys.

"I know!" Mrs. Griffiths smiled, and then something through the window caught her eye. "Someone's out there," she said, "lying on the ground in the snow. Is it Gwyn?"

She opened the window to call to her son but suddenly a shaft of lightning pierced the snow, and with a deafening crack, hit the ground just where Gwyn lay. Mrs. Griffiths screamed and fell to the floor. Eirlys, who had run to her, was the only one to see what happened within the circle of thorn trees.

She saw the ground sparkle and shake, and Gwyn, arms outstretched, being tossed like a bird in the wind. She saw his hands glowing in the snow, and the earth beneath them crack and a shower of glittering icicles fly up and decorate the trees like tinsel. And in one of the trees something shone brighter than a star, and she knew that Arianwen was safe.

Only then did Eirlys run to fetch a cold washcloth. She laid it on Mrs. Griffiths's head and gently stroked her hair.

Mrs. Griffiths opened her eyes. "It's you," she said, and she took the girl's hand. "What happened? I felt strange and so afraid."

"It's the snow," Eirlys replied. "It's the whiteness. It makes you feel strange sometimes."

Mrs. Griffiths sat up, still keeping the girl's hand clasped in hers. "It's so good to have you here," she said.

They stayed quite still for a moment: the girl kneeling beside the woman, calm and silent, until Mrs. Griffiths suddenly got to her feet exclaiming, "What a poor nurse I am! It's you who's supposed to be the patient. Back to bed now or the doctor will be scolding me!"

She had just tucked the girl's blankets in again, when Gwyn appeared in the doorway. He was wet with snow and smiling triumphantly.

"Gwyn! Was that you out there?" his mother asked. "Lying in the snow? Are you crazy?"

"No, not crazy — a magician!" he replied.

Mrs. Griffiths made a clicking noise with her tongue. "I don't know," she said. "Sometimes I wonder if Mrs. Davis wasn't right about you."

"Can I talk to Eirlys for a bit?"

"You ought to be in school," his mother said, "but seeing that you aren't, yes, you can have a chat. Change your clothes first and dry your hair!"

Gwyn retreated. When he returned, dry, to the bedroom, he was carrying his grandmother's black book. "I've got Arianwen," he said, and he held out his hand, allowing the silver spider to crawl onto the patchwork quilt. "I had to fight for her; something was trying to stop me."

"I saw," said Eirlys. "You *are* a magician, Gwyn!"

Gwyn was gratified, yet a little embarrassed. "I've been looking at Nain's book," he told the girl, "and I can read it. I never thought I could."

"Read it to me then, and we'll try and find the demon in the broken horse!"

Gwyn sat on the bed and began to read the old Welsh legends, translating as he went. It was not an easy task, but the more he read, the more fluent he became, and Eirlys heard again the stories that she half-remembered, from the time when Nain had sat where Gwyn was sitting now, and would talk on and on, until she slept.

She heard about kings and princes, magicians and giants, and even the knights of King Arthur, but nowhere could Gwyn find a broken horse.

"Read about Princess Branwen," Eirlys said. "There are horses in that legend, I remember. It used to make me cry, but I've forgotten it."

Gwyn began the story of Branwen. Before he had read two pages he suddenly stopped and said quietly, "I found it. But it is too terrible to read aloud. I can't read it!"

"Tell me," said Eirlys.

"I can't!" Gwyn stared at the page; there were tears in his eyes.

"Tell me!" she insisted.

"You'll hate it," said Gwyn, and then he read, " 'Efnisien, Branwen's brother, came upon the King of Ireland's horses. "Whose horses are these?" he asked. "They belong to the King of Ireland," said the soldiers. "He has come to marry your sister, Branwen." And Efnisien screamed, "No one asked me. No one asked my consent. She shall not marry the King of Ireland!" And he drew his sword, and filled with rage and hatred, he cut off the horses' ears and their tails, their eyelids and their lips, until they screamed with pain, and no one could touch them!' "

Silence filled the room and Gwyn said, "You're sorry now, I told you!"

"No!" Eirlys had drawn the quilt around her neck. "We had to know. Perhaps that crazy prince never died, but became locked in the broken horse because of what he'd done!"

"Nain tried to burn the horse, but she couldn't," said Gwyn.

"It couldn't be destroyed so it was given to the magicians to keep safe," Eirlys suggested. "They were the most powerful men in the land in those days!" She paused and then said, "Well, now you know who you have to catch!"

"I know his name, but I can't see him. How do I know where he is?"

"He's on the mountain, for sure. You'll be able to feel him. And you have Arianwen to help you!"

Gwyn went to the window and drew the curtains wide. It was light now and snowflakes were flying past the window; some would linger in their journey and dance gently up and down against the pane before drifting onto the apple tree below.

"Perhaps you'd better wait," said Eirlys, when she saw the snow. "There'll be a blizzard on the mountain."

"No! I don't dare wait. Something will happen if I don't stop him now. I won't go far. I know what to do. Tell Mom I've gone to see Nain."

Mrs. Griffiths was in the kitchen when Gwyn slipped downstairs, put on his coat and boots, and for the second time that morning, crept out of the house.

He realized, as soon as he was through the door, that he would not get far. Eirlys was right. There was a blizzard on the mountain. The wind and snow lashed his face, and he had to screw up his eyes and look down at his boots in order to make any headway. But he knew the way, and he knew what he had to do.

When he arrived at the stone wall from where he had flung the broken horse, he took Arianwen from his pocket and held her out into the snow. She clung to his hand for a moment, bracing herself against the wind.

"Go!" Gwyn whispered. And then words came to him that he had never known and did not understand, and he began to chant.

The spider rolled off Gwyn's hand and drifted up into the snow. He watched her, shining silver among the white flakes, and then he had to shut his eyes against the blizzard. When he opened them the spider had gone, and already the wind had slackened. There was a sudden stillness as the mountain held its breath. Clouds of snow began to gather on the summit; they intensified and rolled downward in a vast, ever-thickening ice-cold wave. In a few seconds, Gwyn could hardly see his hands. He felt for the stone wall and found instead, something smooth and tall — a pillar of ice!

And then Gwyn ran — or rather threw himself, blind from the snow and stumbling, down the track and away from his spell. Arianwen had begun to spin!

❄ ❄ ❄

At that moment, someone was knocking on the farmhouse door. Mrs. Griffiths, when she opened it, found Alun Lloyd on the doorstep.

"It is Alun, isn't it?" she asked, for the boy was muffled up to his eyes in a thick red scarf.

"Yes," Alun mumbled through the scarf.

"You didn't go to school?"

"No school," the reply was just audible. "No bus — blizzard — where's Gwyn?"

"Stamp the snow off those boots and come in!" said Mrs. Griffiths. She took the boy's coat and shook it outside before closing the door. "Gwyn's upstairs with the girl," she went on. "Poor little thing had an accident yesterday. She's in bed!"

"I heard," muttered Alun. "Can I go up?"

" 'Course, Love. First door on the left. Don't stay too long, though. She's still a little —"

Alun had sprung up the stairs before Mrs. Griffiths could finish her sentence. He opened the door and saw only the girl. She was sitting up in bed, reading a book.

"Where's Gwyn?" Alun asked.

"With his grandmother," the girl replied.

"No, he's not. I've been there!"

The two children stared at each other across the patterned quilt.

Alun decided to put his question another way. "Is he in the house? Won't he see me?"

The girl regarded him gravely, and he had to look away from her strange, greeny-blue gaze. He did not like her eyes; they made him feel cold.

"OK. You're not going to tell, are you? I'm sorry about — about your falling down and that, and I came to say so." He glanced briefly at her pale face, then quickly averted his eyes again. "But I want to tell Gwyn about it. I want to talk to him, see? And I'm going to find him. I don't care if it takes — forever!"

Alun turned swiftly and ran out of the room.

A few seconds later, Mrs. Griffiths heard the front door slam and called out, "Was that Alun? Why didn't he stay?" Receiving no reply, she returned to her laundry, still unaware that Gwyn was not in the house.

Outside, Alun saw footsteps in the snow, and began to follow them.

❄ ❄ ❄

Gwyn returned only minutes later, and having quietly divested himself of snow-soaked garments, crept barefoot up to the bedroom.

"It's done!" he told Eirlys. "The spell's begun!"

"Your friend was here!" she said.

"Alun? What did he want?"

"To see you! He was angry!"

"Where did he go?" Gwyn began to feel a terrible apprehension overwhelming him.

"I think he went onto the mountain," Eirlys replied with equal consternation.

"I didn't see him. He must have missed the track!"

"He'll get lost!"

"Trapped!" cried Gwyn. "Trapped and frozen!" He tore down the stairs and out into the snow, forgetting in his panic, to put on his boots or his coat or to shut the front door. He called his friend's name, again and again as he ran, until he was hoarse. The snow had become a fog, still and heavy, like a blanket, smothering any sound.

He found his way with difficulty to the place where he had touched the pillar of ice. There was another beside it now, and another and another. They rose higher than he could reach and too close to pass through. A wall of ice! Gwyn beat on the wall, he kicked it, tore at it with his fingers, all the while calling Alun's name in his feeble croaking voice, and then he slid to the ground, defeated by his own spell.

CHAPTER NINE

Return

GWYN'S MOTHER WAS WAITING FOR HIM WHEN HE STUMBLED home. "You left the door open," she accused him. "What have you been doing? Where's Alun?"

Gwyn could not tell her. The trap had been set and now there was nothing anyone could do until Arianwen had finished her work. Besides, Alun might have gone home; they had no proof that he was on the mountain. "I think he's gone home," Gwyn told his mother.

But later that day, when Mr. Lloyd arrived, searching for his eldest son, Gwyn admitted, "Yes! Alun was here," and, "Yes! He might have gone onto the mountain. But I don't know. I don't know for sure!"

Then Mrs. Lloyd, who had followed her husband with little Iolo, rounded on Gwyn and vented all her anger and her fear upon him. "He was your friend," she cried. "He came to look for you! Why didn't you go after him? Why didn't you say something? Don't you remember how it was when your sister went? It's been four hours now! Don't you care? Don't you care about anyone, Gwyn Griffiths? You're not normal! Not a normal boy at all!"

Little Iolo began to scream, and Gwyn's fingers ached with the desire to hurt. But he could not use his power because he knew the woman was terribly afraid. How could she know that he was suffering as much as she? He left the kitchen and went up to his room.

He could see nothing out of his window, the fog was so dense. He knew he had to protect Alun, but how? And then he remembered something Nain had said about those long-ago magicians. They could "turn men into eagles"! Why couldn't he turn Alun into a bird — a small bird — white so that it should not be seen against the snow.

He scanned the room for something that had belonged to Alun and saw, on his bookshelf, an old paperback on boats that his friend had lent him. It hardly seemed appropriate but it would have to do. He took the book to the window and held it very tight. He closed his eyes and tried to see Alun, tried to remember every feature of his friend: his blue eyes and his freckles, and his short red fingers with the nails all bitten. And then he thought of a bird, a small white bird, and put the picture of the bird that was in his mind over the blue eyes, the freckled nose, and the tufty blond hair of his friend, until the bird and the boy seemed to become one.

Gwyn did not know how long he stood by the window. He was not aware of any sound until the search party began to arrive. The grapevine in Pendewi worked fast; sometimes people even sensed the news before they heard it. Ten men set off to look for Alun Lloyd, and later Mrs. Griffiths and another wife followed them.

The search did not last long. Gwyn heard them return: the defeated stamping of boots in the snow, the grave, deep voices, and the kettle whistling on and on and on!

Hunger and curiosity drove him downstairs. The kitchen was so crowded he could not find a chair, nor reach the bread bin. He managed to sneak a plate of cookies from the table and retreated with it to the door, where he leaned and listened, waiting for someone to mention the mountain and whatever it was that Arianwen had built there.

They were all talking at once, yet avoiding what they wanted to say. They were adults and did not know how to discuss something that was impossible, something they did not understand.

There were pools of water on the kitchen floor, mingling with crushed cookies. Iolo was under the table, sniffling, but everyone had become accustomed to the sound and was ignoring him. And Gwyn remembered that other search, four years ago, when he had sat under the table and cried because his sister was lost.

And then the words that he wanted to hear began to creep out toward him.

"Did you feel it?" "Very peculiar!" "Like a net!" "A cloud?" "No, not that!" "Ice!" "A frozen cloud?" "More like a wall!" "Never heard of anything like it!" "Call the police!" "What can they do?" "Can't see a thing out there!" "Searchlights?"

Gwyn sidled out the door and carried his plate of cookies upstairs. He heard the police arrive and the girl, being the last person to see Alun, was called down to speak to them.

Everybody stopped talking when she came in. They drew back and gazed at the frail, white-faced child, so insubstantial and fairylike in her white nightgown and borrowed gray shawl. They were all thinking about that other time, in the same farm-house, when they had come to search for a girl like this one, so very like this one. Only the other had been dark and rosy-cheeked, and they had never found her. They bent their heads, straining to hear the words the girl spoke so softly. And when she had finished, they all began to sigh and murmur about mists and mountains, and Officer Perkins had to erase half his notes. He was new to the area, just up from the city, and he felt like a stranger among these superstitious and excitable farmers; their melodious voices conveyed nothing but confusion to him.

He went out, all the same, with his partner, Officer Price, and they walked up the track for a bit, to find out what they could. They returned before long, and drove away without a word.

It'll be in the papers, thought Gwyn. *They'll call it a phenomenon, and then they'll forget about it!*

The searchers departed in ones and twos. "We'll be back in the morning!" they called. "We'll find him!"

The Lloyds were the last to leave. Iolo had fallen asleep in his father's arms, but now Mrs. Lloyd was crying.

It was such a long, long night. Gwyn could not sleep. He sat on the edge of his bed and stared at the window. Eirlys came up and kept him company. They did not speak but her presence was comforting. Just as she was about to go, a sound came from the mountain: a long, wailing sigh!

"Did you hear that?" Gwyn whispered.

"Was it the wind?" she asked.

"No, not the wind!"

The sound came again. Louder this time. Such an anguished, melancholy howl. It crept down Gwyn's spine and made him shiver.

"It's like a wild animal," said Eirlys.

"Trapped!" he added.

The howling gradually died away, and Eirlys returned to her bed. But, later that night it came again, louder and more terrible than ever, though it seemed to be only Gwyn who heard it. It got into his head, and he had to rock back and forth to endure the sound. He knew who it was, of course, and agonized over what it might do to Alun if it found him.

And then he became aware that the sound was in the room; it was in the silver pipe, lying on the bedside table.

Gwyn jumped out of bed, seized the pipe, and ran with it across the room, thrusting it into his drawer and slamming the drawer tight after it. But to his horror, the voice within the drawer seemed to intensify; it got louder and louder until the whole chest vibrated with the sound.

Gwyn put his hands over his ears and stumbled backward to the bed. *It knows about the pipe,* Gwyn thought. *It's using it to fight me. But it won't get out! It won't! It won't! It won't! Arianwen and I are too strong for it!*

It ended at last. Gwyn lay back, exhausted, and fell asleep on top of the bed sheets.

He was awakened by another sound: a muffled, intermittent tapping on his window. Someone was throwing snowballs.

He went to the window, opened it, and looked out. There was a shadowy figure beside the apple tree, but he could not make out any of its features. "Who's there?" he called.

"Alun!" came the reply.

Gwyn ran down and opened the front door.

Alun was standing in the porch. He was pale, but certainly not frozen. He was holding something small and dark in his hand, and he had an odd, vacant expression in his eyes, as though he was not sure why or how he had come to be there. He stepped into the house, and when the door had been closed behind him, he wordlessly followed Gwyn into the kitchen, where he laid the thing that he had been holding on the kitchen table. It was the broken horse!

Gwyn stared at it. "Where've you been?" he asked gently.

"Out there!" Alun jerked his head toward the window.

"I know, out there," said Gwyn, "but where?"

Alun wiped his nose on the sleeve of his coat. He did not seem inclined to answer any more questions.

"Better take some of that off," said Gwyn, nodding at his friend's soaking clothes.

Alun removed his coat, his boots, and his socks, and then he sank onto a kitchen chair and wiped his nose, this time on his shirt cuff.

"Wish you would tell me about it!" Gwyn bit his lip. He realized that it was no use trying to force Alun to talk. He would have to wait until his friend was ready.

Alun scratched his head. "I dunno. It's all so peculiar. I don't really understand what happened. I was following your footsteps in that blizzard and I got lost. So I turned around to come back — and I couldn't. There was something there, like bars: They were ice cold, but hard as anything. At first it was all cloudy, and I couldn't see, but then it got brighter and brighter and I saw what I was caught in. It was a sort of cage, bars all around in a pattern, like a . . . like a . . ."

"Cobweb?" Gwyn suggested.

"Phew!" Alun looked hard at Gwyn. "You know, don't you? It's funny, though. All those things you said — they were true, weren't they?"

"Yes, they were true!"

"Well, I suppose you know about the man, then?"

"What man?" Gwyn stepped closer. "Was there a man in there with you?"

"A kind of man. He scared me. He had red hair and he was dressed in all kinds of bright stuff: jewelry and that, with a cloak and a gold belt with a big sword in it. And he was beating at the bars with his fists, tearing at them, banging his head on them, and yelling. I was scared. But he didn't see me. It sounds funny but I felt very small and kind of . . . like I had something around me, something very warm and soft. Anyway, he kept on and on at those bars for hours and hours. I fell asleep, and when I woke up he was still at it: moaning and crying, and then something awful happened!"

Gwyn waited. He could hardly bear the suspense but he dared not ask a question.

"He began to disappear," Alun continued, "just shrank, sort of faded away, and so did the bars of ice, until there was nothing left there, except . . ."

"Except what?"

"That!" Alun pointed to the broken horse.

Gwyn looked at it, lying on its side, black and disfigured. *Poor thing!* he thought. *You want so much to get out: but I can never, never let you.* It was all over, and suddenly he felt very tired.

There were sounds from above and Gwyn said, "They've been looking for you — your dad and mine."

"I bet!" said Alun.

"And Mr. Davis came, and Gary Pritchard's dad, and Mr. Ellis, and Mr. Jones, and people I can't remember. Even Mrs. Pritchard came, and she and my mom went out to look. And your mom was here with Iolo, I don't know why she brought him. He was making such a racket."

"He always does." Alun nodded sympathetically.

Mrs. Griffiths came into the kitchen and gasped at the sight of Alun, sitting there, so rosy and cheerful, but before she could utter a word, the doorbell rang. The Lloyds had returned to resume their search.

Mrs. Griffiths ran to open the door. "He's back," she cried. "He's safe. Good as new and nothing wrong with him, as far as I can see."

"Where? Where?" Mrs. Lloyd tore into the kitchen and flung herself upon her son.

"Come on, Mom. I'm OK," came Alun's muffled voice from beneath his mother.

"What happened? Where've you been? They went to search. We thought you'd freeze!"

"I stayed where I was." Alun said, wriggling. "I didn't want to get lost. I got behind some rocks — in a sort of cave. It was very warm, really."

Mrs. Lloyd began to wrap up her boy like a baby, though the mist had gone and the sky was brightening. She bundled him out into the hallway, talking nonstop and nervously to her husband and Mrs. Griffiths. And while she spoke, Alun looked back at Gwyn and said, "I found this out there, as well," and he put something cool into Gwyn's hand — the snow spider.

Gwyn curled his fingers around the spider as Alun whispered hoarsely, "Don't tell about . . . about what I said, will you?"

"I won't tell!" Gwyn grinned. "One nutcase is enough!"

Alun grinned back and gave the thumbs-up sign, before his mother whisked him through the door.

❄ ❄ ❄

Mr. Griffiths had his way, and Eirlys stayed for Christmas. It was the sort of Christmas one always remembers. The trees were iced with snow, and the sun came out to make the mountain sparkle. The biggest Christmas tree they had ever seen at Tŷ Bryn was put into the front room, and decorated with lights like candles, with silver stars and homemade sweets wrapped in colored paper.

A log fire was lit and they all played Monopoly and Scrabble, and even made-up games, so as to prolong the fun. Mrs. Griffiths played carols on the out-of-tune piano with damp hammers, and it did not matter that the soloists were sometimes out of tune, too. The children giggled at Nain, who looked like a Christmas tree herself, all bedecked in colored beads and bangles.

Just before they went to bed, Eirlys looked out of the window at the white, moonlit mountain and said, "It reminds me of home!" Only Gwyn heard her. He knew that she was not talking about Wales and it occurred to him, for the first time, that she might not stay with them forever.

On New Year's Day, the children decided to walk in the fields. It was a cold day, and while the girl waited in the garden, Gwyn ran up to get the gloves his father had given him for Christmas. They were blue and silver, lined with fur, and Gwyn cherished them even more than his black watch.

When he opened his drawer, he saw Arianwen and the silver pipe. They looked so innocent, who would guess what they could do? One that had traveled a million miles or more, the other from somewhere in the distant past. They would always be with him now, he knew that. As he turned away the pipe whispered something — it sounded like, "Don't go!" Gwyn smiled and put on his gloves, "I'm not going anywhere!" he said.

His parents were outside in the garden with Eirlys. They were standing by the gate, talking quietly while they stared up at the mountain. They did not see Gwyn when he came out, nor hear him close the front door.

"I have to go soon," he heard Eirlys say. "I have to go back to where I came from."

His parents did not speak immediately. They seemed to have been frozen by her remark, and then Mrs. Griffiths put her hand out and gently tucked the girl's hair into her hood, saying, "Do you have to go, Eirlys? Can't you stay?"

Eirlys shook her head.

"Were you happy there, where you came from?" Mr. Griffiths asked.

"Oh, yes! Very happy!"

They did not ask where she lived; they did not seem to want to know. And then Gwyn broke into their thoughts. "Come on," he cried, "I'll race you to the trees!" and he ran past them through the open gate.

Eirlys followed, and they ran to the circle of hawthorn trees, where Gwyn had released Arianwen. The snow had melted and the grass was smooth and green. There was nothing to show that the earth had shaken or that icicles had flown from it, like stars.

"Why couldn't she escape without my help?" Gwyn thought aloud. "She has her own power."

"She has nothing without you," said Eirlys. "She needs your thoughts to help her."

"She's just an ordinary spider, then?"

"Oh no! No creature from my place is a common anything!"

My place! There it was again. "Are you leaving here?" He put the question cautiously.

"Today!" she answered.

"What? So soon? You can't!"

"They are coming for me!" She looked up at the sky. "Even with your magic, I only had until today."

"Do you want to go?"

"Oooooh yes!" Her reply came like a deep contented sigh.

"But Mom and Dad?"

"They understand. I said I had to go back to where I came from."

Gwyn nodded. "They don't want to know the truth," he said.

"I think they do know. But they're too old now to be able to talk about it."

"And they don't mind you leaving?"

She shook her head and smiled at him. "It'll be all right now between you and Dad. He knows I'm safe. That's all he wanted."

"And the Herberts?"

"I'm just a number that got muddled up. They think I've left already."

They began to walk up the track without his really being aware of it. When they passed the first bend and the farm disappeared from sight, Gwyn suddenly stopped to look at a falcon hanging motionless in the air. Cloud shadows raced across the snowcapped mountains beyond the bird, and a truck, piled with golden hay, made its way slowly across the green fields below.

"Won't you miss all this?" Gwyn asked.

"No!" she said. "I like it where I'm going."

He noticed the cold before he saw anything. "I don't think I'll come any farther," he said.

"Come on! Just for a bit, to keep me company!" She took his hand.

Her fingers seemed colder than ever, but he allowed himself to be led away from the track and through the fields of sheep. And then he saw the light, glinting now and then, through the billows of a great, gray cloud. And he felt an icy breeze on his face.

"You go on," he said. "I'm staying here!" He tried to pull his hand away, but she would not let him. They were approaching the flat field where Bethan had gone to rescue the black ewe four years before.

"Let me go!" cried Gwyn.

Her fingers tightened on his wrist. He twisted and turned but her grip was like steel, her strength irresistible. He could see the ship now, falling slowly through the clouds, the great sail swelling, the dancing creatures sparkling on the hull. Icy fragments spun earthward, and terrified sheep swung away from the field and scattered in a great wave past the children.

"Let me go!" Gwyn begged.

"Come with me!" Her soft voice floated above the moan of the wind, "Come!"

"No!" Gwyn screamed. "I want to stay. No! No! No! Leave me!"

"Come!" She looked back at him and smiled, but her fingers bit deeper into his wrist. "Please!" She sighed. "I need you, Gwyn. We need you — out there!"

"No!" Gwyn began to shake and through his tears, saw the ship as a huge, glittering cloud behind the girl's pale shape. Then a voice inside him suddenly burst out, "Gwydion lives HERE!" and he tore from her grasp and flung himself to the ground.

He lay there, with his eyes closed, nursing his aching hand, and when the bitter cold and all the threatening sounds had vanished, he got up and saw something where Eirlys had been — the yellow scarf, frozen into the snow, and the seaweed beside it. He picked them up and put the seaweed into his pocket, but the scarf was stiff with frost, like a strange, twisted stick.

He wandered slowly through the fields until he came to the track and there, on the last bend, he found Alun standing by the stone wall.

"What's that?" Alun asked.

"Someone's scarf," said Gwyn. "Look, it's still frozen!"

"Where's the girl?"

"She's gone!"

"Phew!" said Alun.

They walked back to the farm in comfortable silence. Mr. Griffiths was standing in the porch when they arrived. "She's gone?" he said.

"Yes!" Gwyn replied. And then, before his father could turn away, he said, "I'm not going, Dad. I'm not ever going!"

"I know!" Mr. Griffiths smiled. "And I'm glad of that, Gwyn! Very glad!"

They went into the house. A house that was not empty anymore.

Read the first chapter of

EMLYN'S MOON

THE MAGICIAN TRILOGY

BOOK TWO

Coming January 2007

CHAPTER ONE
The Boy from the Chapel

"DON'T GO INTO LLEWELYN'S CHAPEL!" THEY TOLD NIA. "NO good will come of it. Something happened there!" But Nia disobeyed. If she hadn't, nothing would have changed. She'd still be plain Nia, dull Nia, Nia who couldn't do anything!

❊ ❊ ❊

It all began on the day they left Tŷ Llŷr. The children, tucked between boxes in the back of the Land Rover, were waiting for their mother to lock up. Nia was propped up on a rolled mattress at the open end of the car. She was gazing at a red geranium in the kitchen window, the only bright thing left. And then the flower was lifted out of the dark window by unseen hands. It reappeared in the doorway, perched upon a pile of towels in her mother's arms.

"I nearly forgot it!" Mrs. Lloyd beamed over the geranium.

Nia wished she *had* forgotten the flower, just for a day or two. At least there would have been something left alive in Tŷ Llŷr. If a house could look forlorn, then that's how Tŷ Llŷr seemed to her: curtains gone from the windows, the farmyard bare and tidy, and a stillness so unnatural it almost hurt. A stray feather drifted in the sunlight, the only reminder that chickens had once inhabited the yard. It was May but the ewes and their lambs were gone, and the only sounds came from bees in the giant sycamore tree.

Even the children in the Land Rover were silent. Leaving their home had ceased to be an exciting idea; suddenly it had become a rather shocking reality.

Mrs. Lloyd climbed up to sit beside her husband. The engine started. The spell was broken. An excited shouting and chattering broke out.

Nia was the only one to look back and see the boy beneath the sycamore. He was standing so close to the shadowy tree trunk that she could barely make out his shape. But she knew it was Gwyn Griffiths by the mass of dark hair and the way he stood, his hands in his pockets, so very still and thoughtful. No other boy could do that.

Nia nudged her brother, wedged in beside her. "Look, Alun! There's Gwyn!"

There was so much noise, so much movement among the seven children packed tightly together between boxes and cases, that Alun neither felt nor heard Nia, so she raised her own hand and waved, rather tentatively.

The boy beneath the tree responded.

"He's waving, Alun!" Nia shouted above the rumpus.

"What? Who?"

"Gwyn!"

"Oh!"

"He came to say good-bye, Alun! Quick!"

Alun leaned over his sister, accidentally knocking the sheep-dog's nose with his elbow. Fly yelped, the Land Rover lurched around a bend, and Alun was flung backward on top of his twin brothers. Siôn and Gareth were too happy to grumble.

Gwyn Griffiths disappeared from sight.

The Land Rover rattled on down the mountain, gathering speed as the lane became steeper, and the chatter in the back increased to a hysterical crescendo of excitement. Catrin even broke into song.

Mr. Lloyd joined in, humming gustily. He'd done it at last: broken free of the farm that his ailing father-in-law had begged him to take over. Iestyn Lloyd was a small, dark man, his face as weather-tanned as any hill farmer, but he was too fond of his food to stay as fit as he should, too gregarious to enjoy the solitary existence that suited his neighbor Ivor Griffiths so well. But he had tried, no one could say he hadn't. For fifteen years he'd struggled with hard mountain earth, with ewes trapped in snow and lambs lost, and he had failed. He would never make a good farmer — his heart wasn't in it — and with another child on the way, he had to find some way of earning a decent living. When the butcher's shop in Pendewi came up for sale, it was like an answer to Iestyn's prayers. He'd been an apprentice butcher, it was what he knew, what he could do best. He would succeed this time. He'd sold his stock and all his land to Ivor Griffiths, who had a magic touch when it came to animals, and a way of knowing the land that only a born farmer could have.

No one wanted the farmhouse, though. No one wanted

ancient Tŷ Llŷr, with its crumbling chimney, its family of bats, and the plum trees that curled their way under the wavy roof.

"Mae hen wlad fy nhadau yn annwyl i mi," sang Mr. Lloyd, breaking out in a rare exhibition of patriotism, as he cheerfully sped away from the things that Nia loved.

Fly, the sheepdog, rolled her eyes and gazed imploringly at Nia. The dog, at least, felt as apprehensive as she.

There was nothing in Pendewi for Nia. She had neither the talents nor the aspirations of her brothers and sisters. In Pendewi there was a library for Nerys to browse in every day, if she wished. For Catrin, there was a music teacher only two doors away, and a disco on Saturdays. For the boys, there were shops stuffed with comics and bubble gum, with batteries and nails, glue and string. There they would all be, crammed into their little rooms above the shop, reading and singing, building, hammering, and chewing, while the plums turned from green to gold in the orchard at Tŷ Llŷr and strangers put them into baskets and carried them away.

No one would notice the wild Welsh poppies that Nia had nurtured in little places by the stream, or see the white roses behind the farmhouse. The garden would become a carpet of petals, and then, when the wind came, the petals would scatter over the mountain like snow. And no one seemed to care, not even Mrs. Lloyd, preoccupied as she was with thoughts of the baby who would come in summer, when the plums were turning gold.

Gwyn Griffiths's sister had loved flowers, but she had vanished on the mountain. No one knew how this had come about.

"I wish you had waved to Gwyn!" Nia said to Alun, but she spoke half to herself and did not expect him to hear.

The Land Rover slowed down before turning onto the main road. Summer visitors had begun to arrive and the road was busy. Mr. Lloyd swung in behind a camping trailer, and there they stayed, unable to pass the clumsy vehicle, traveling so slowly that Nia could count the primroses on the edge of the road.

At the top of the hill leading down into Pendewi, the trailer stopped without warning. Mr. Lloyd jammed on his brakes and leaned out of the window, mouthing oaths about visitors and trailers; he could see the owner in the driver's seat of his smart red car, unconcernedly reading a map. Mr. Lloyd banged his fist on the horn. The children pressed forward, anticipating a fight, all except for Nia, who had noticed something far more interesting.

The Land Rover had stopped beside the old chapel; the chapel that wasn't a chapel now, but a home for someone. The gate and the iron railings had been painted pink and gold, the door was blue with big golden flowers on it, and bright curtains framed the long windows. When Nia stood up she could see down into the room beyond the window. A boy in green trousers lay sprawled across a rug; he was doing something with his hands — making something — but Nia couldn't see what it was. Curious, she leaned farther out, but as she did so, the Land Rover suddenly jerked forward. Nia screamed and clutched wildly at the air, trying to keep her balance.

The boy in the chapel looked up in surprise, and then grinned at Nia's predicament before Alun caught the back of her sweater and pulled her to safety.

"What on earth were you doing?" Nerys, the eldest, inquired irritably. She felt responsible for incidents in the back of the Land Rover.

"I was just looking," Nia replied.

"Looking at what?"

"Just into the chapel. I saw Emlyn Llewelyn from school. I didn't know he lived there!"

"Of course he does," said Alun. "He and his dad. That chapel's a bad place!"

"Who says?"

"Gwyn says!"

"Why?"

"Something happened there." Alun said.

"What happened?" Nia persisted.

"I dunno — something bad! There's something all wrong about that place. No one goes there!"

"It's beautiful!" Nia protested. "And I like Emlyn."

"You don't know, do you?" Alun said in a grim and rather condescending manner.

Nia was silent. Why had she defended Emlyn? She hardly knew him. He was in Alun's class and nearly two years older than she was. She wished she had been able to see farther into his strange home.

Outside Pendewi, the trailer turned left onto the seaside road, and the Land Rover continued on, down into the little market town.

Sunshine flooded High Street. The trees were in blossom, and Saturday shoppers in bright spring clothes bustled in and out of the narrow gray-tiled houses. *It isn't such a bad place after all,* Nia thought.

The Lloyds parked outside a tall black-and-white building at the farthest end of the town. There was a huge blue van in front of them, with moving company men in gray overalls munching sandwiches in the cab of the truck. The furniture was all in place.

There were two entrances: one that led into a shop furbished with red carcasses and neat trays of sliced meat; the other, a very private-looking black door with a brass number 6 on it.

The family went into their new home through the black, private door, leaving it open to allow warmth and light into the dark house.

Mr. Lloyd persuaded the reluctant and grumbling Fly to go down a long passage to the backyard. Mrs. Lloyd sank into a sunny chair by the door; she was still carrying the red geranium.

The four boys clattered noisily up the stairs and along the creaking and uncarpeted landing, eager to open boxes that had been closed up for weeks — to find ancient and beloved toys and strew them across floorboards of unfamiliar rooms and make the place theirs, their fortress and their home.

Nerys, Nia, and Catrin stood in front of their mother, who was flushed and pretty in her flowery apron.

"Well, I think we should go upstairs first, girls. When the clothes are in the drawers and the beds are made, we'll have a cup of tea."

Nia followed her older sisters upstairs. Nerys and Catrin

disappeared into a room overlooking High Street. Nia glimpsed a wide, sunlit window before the door was closed against her.

Opposite her sisters' room, Siôn, Gareth, and Alun had already extended their territory. A wooden railroad track snaked through their open door and along the landing. Nia sidestepped, but it was too late! She tripped and a red engine flew across the floor.

"Watch it!" the twins sang out. "'Nia Can't Do Nothing!' 'Nia in the Middle!' Nia's got a funny tooth, and her nose goes squiggle, squiggle!"

Nia was fed up with the twins' new rhyme, but she couldn't think of a suitably clever retort. It was all true, of course — that was the worst of it. They'd got her, pinned her down like a butterfly on a board, only she was more of a moth — a very ordinary brown moth who wasn't good at anything except screwing up her nose when she didn't understand something. A moth in the middle, who had two butterfly sisters, an older brother who could fix anything, two younger brothers who could stand on their heads, and an even younger one who got by just because he was the youngest and had curls.

She retrieved the red engine and put it into Siôn's hand. "It's Iolo's engine, anyway," she said.

The twins allowed Nia to escape without further aggravation. She continued down the hall until she reached two open doors at the end. To her left was the the bathroom, bright with sunlight and frosted glass. Iolo was playing with something in the tub: Little waves of soapy water were spilling over onto the floor.

Let someone else find the puddle! Leaving Iolo in peace, Nia turned to the room on her right, the room she was to share with Iolo. There were no spaces left for her in her sisters' room and none for Iolo in his brothers'. They would have to put up with each other for the time being. As they had grown in size and number, the Lloyd children had become used to an annual re-arrangement of bedrooms. If the new baby was a girl, Nia would share the baby's bright little room at the top of the house, if it was a boy, Iolo would move in with the new brother, and Nia would stay here in this small, shadowy room that had an old and unused air about it.

The window looked out onto the backyard, a yard in shadow with hardly a blade of grass. There was the river to look at, though, splashing over bleached pebbles beyond the wall enclosing the yard. And on the other side of the river, Morgan the Smithy's long black barn with blue sparks lighting the windows, and Morgan and his sons singing in green coveralls.

Next year, there would be flowers growing by the river. Nia fumbled in her pockets and brought out a tiny paper package. She carefully unfolded the paper and laid on the floor a part of Tŷ Llŷr: honesty seeds in their flat, silvery shells, and tiny black poppy and campion seeds, all mixed together, so that when she sowed them next spring, the meager little patch below would be splashed with orange and purple and pink.

"What's that?" Iolo had finished with boats and stood dripping in the doorway.

"Seeds," Nia replied. "You'd better dry yourself and the floor, or you'll get in trouble."

"I can't find a towel," Iolo explained.

Nia could hear her mother moving around in the room above them. "I'll look downstairs for you. Mom had them in the hall."

"I need something to eat, too," Iolo informed her.

"I'll see."

Nia tucked her precious seeds back into a pocket and went downstairs.

Sunlight was streaming through a semicircle of stained glass above the front door. The hall was lined with a clutter of cases, bags, and upturned chairs, but in the center there was only one thing: a box, *the* box! Nia recognized it; it contained Mom's clothes from twenty years ago: dresses that were too tight but too full of memories to throw away, shoes that were too flimsy, and beads too bright for a mother of seven. It was like a gift, wrapped in the glowing colors from the stained-glass window. A gift for "Nia Can't Do Nothing," who could now become "Nia Can Do Anything!"

Forgetting Iolo and towels, Nia knelt beside the box and began to pick at the string that held it shut. The string fell off and she opened the box. Almost reverently she began to lift out the contents and lay them on the floor.

There were shouts from above and around Nia, but amazingly, no one came into the hall. Catrin had found the piano and was practicing her scales. Fly was whining somewhere.

"Someone take the dog out!" Mr. Lloyd shouted from the shop.

No one answered.

Nia had found a violet dress, patterned with pink-and-white

flowers. She stood up and slipped it over her head. The hem touched the ground. She knelt again and rummaged around in the box, trying to find the thing she needed. There it was — a wide-brimmed red straw hat. And now she could feel the little paper bundles of beads and shoes at the bottom of the box. She drew out a rope of big silver shells and a pair of pink shoes with stars on them.

Nia kicked off her sneakers and stepped into the pink shoes. The violet dress covered them, she would trip. The silver shells would have to become a belt. They encircled her waist perfectly, not a shell too long. Nia hitched the dress a few inches over the shell belt, just enough to reveal the shoes. She was almost ready.

The finishing touch was a long string of multicolored beads wound once, twice, three times around her neck.

Catrin moved on from Mendelssohn to Mozart, and Fly's distant whine became a long, low howl.

"Someone take that poor dog for a walk," Mrs. Lloyd pleaded from a box-lined room upstairs.

"I'll go," answered Nia.

"Don't let her off the leash; she's not used to the town," came a voice muffled by mounds of linen. "And don't go into any shops."

"I won't!"

"Poor thing! She can't stay here much longer." The rest of Mrs. Lloyd's words were drowned out by Fly's howl of agreement.

Nia tottered down the hall and opened the back door. Four

stone steps led down into the yard. Fly was tied to the rail beside the steps, with just enough leash to allow her to stretch out, head on paws, in a tiny patch of sunlight that had managed to creep around the house. The dog leaped up when she saw Nia and barked joyfully.

"Shhh!" Nia knew her father would not approve of her outfit if he saw her. She began to untie Fly's leash, all the while eyeing the long room that extended into the yard beyond the rest of the house: the hateful room that held all those dead and dreadful things. Through the tiny window she glimpsed a red carcass swinging where her father had just hung it. Mr. Lloyd was whistling, happy among his sides of beef, his lamb chops and purple pigs' livers. Poor dead, dismembered creatures. It was enough to put you off meat forever.

"Ugh!" Nia could even smell them.

Fly, free at last, bounded up the back steps and into the house, dragging Nia behind her. They flew down the hall, Fly scattering discarded cardboard and Nia sliding and tripping in the oversize pink shoes.

Nerys appeared at the top of the stairs, alerted by the commotion. "Nia, what are you . . . ?"

But Nia had opened the front door and leaped through it before her sister had time to take in her appearance.

Fly began to live up to her name: Her paws barely touched the ground as she joyfully flew down the street.

The pink shoes hadn't a chance — the first one flew off and then the other. Nia didn't dare stop to retrieve them for fear of choking Fly. Clasping the red hat to her head with her free hand, she careered after the dog, darting between startled shoppers and shouts of "Watch it!" "Where are you going, girl?" "What's she doing?"

Not a very favorable first appearance, Nia thought.

Fly bounded on, back toward Tŷ Llŷr and the mountain fields. The road became steeper, and at the end of the town, the dog stopped and stared mournfully up the hill, her sides heaving and her long tongue hanging out like a wet flag.

Nia dropped down beside Fly, in worse shape than the dog. They sat side-by-side on the hot pavement, gasping and panting. Nia felt as though she'd spent a month in the desert. She closed her eyes and leaned against Fly's woolly neck. When she opened them again a few moments later, she found herself looking at a shop window and at a boy moving past the window and into the shop. He was a tall boy with thick brown-gold hair and green trousers — the boy from the chapel.

Afterward, Nia could never remember whether it was thirst or curiosity that led her to follow him. Whatever it was, she forgot all the rules, all the warnings about sheepdogs in shops, and followed Emlyn Llewelyn through the door.

The wide back of a woman dressed in brown obliterated most of the counter. The wide woman was whispering to the shopkeeper, a man in red suspenders and a grubby shirt, who seemed more interested in gossip than in business. Nia had time to contemplate the rows of sweets and cookies before making a decision. She spied cans of fruit juice on the highest shelf. On the other side of the shop, Emlyn Llewelyn was bending over tubes of glue.

"Yes?" The shopkeeper was staring suspiciously at Nia.

The wide woman had rolled back, propping herself up on the counter; she was staring at Nia's bare feet.

Nia tried to smile but instead screwed up her nose.

"I want a drink, please!" she said quickly.

"Get what you want then. Can you reach?"

"I think so." Nervous of the disapproving glances, Nia thoughtlessly let the loop of Fly's leash slip down her arm and reached for a can of orange juice. Just as her fingertips touched the can, two more customers entered the shop. Fly panicked: She leaped away from the shelves, growling anxiously. Nia was jerked backward, her heel caught in the hem of the violet dress, and she tumbled to the floor, followed by a pile of cans. Suddenly the whole top shelf became possessed. Cans and bottles tottered and clinked and began to roll toward her. There was nothing Nia could do to halt the dreadful and inexorable shower of cans. Some fell on top of her, some crashed to the floor, and others were caught by a darting figure in green trousers. She was aware of the shopkeeper hopping up and down beside her, kicking at the barking Fly and screaming, "Who's going to pay? Look at the shop!" and low voices murmuring, "It shouldn't be allowed!" "She's not wearing shoes!" "And look at the hat!" "What's her mom thinking of?" "Get the dog out!" "No shoes! No shoes!"

And then a boy's voice said, "It isn't a crime, not wearing shoes!" and Emlyn Llewelyn stepped forward, holding Fly tight by the collar. "Only two cans are damaged," he said, "and we'll buy those. Come on!" He tapped Nia on the shoulder and held out his free hand.

Nia looked up. Emlyn had never spoken to her before. He had golden eyes, like a lion.

"Come on!" commanded Emlyn Llewelyn.

Nia put her hand in his, and he helped her to her feet.

"You'd better hold on to your dog," he said, "and pull your dress up or you'll trip again."

Nia obeyed, and Emlyn placed a pile of coins on the counter. Then he strode out of the shop, dragging Nia with him.

"I owe you for the drink," said Nia when the door had been closed against reproachful mutterings.

"That's OK!" Emlyn said. "Are you all right?"

"Yes," Nia lied. Her shins ached where the cans had hit them. "But I'm thirsty."

"Have one on me." Emlyn held out a can. "The dog looks thirsty, too. It's a nice dog. What's its name?"

"Fly," Nia replied, "and it's a she." She opened the can and tipped it to her lips, gulping and coughing as the drink trickled down her throat.

Emlyn watched her for a moment, politely refraining from mentioning the splutters, then asked, "Why don't you bring Fly over to my place and give her a drink?"

"I don't think I'd better," Nia said. "I have to find Mom's shoes. They fell off when I was running, and they've got stars on them."

"OK!" Emlyn accepted her refusal almost too fast, as though he expected it. He kicked the ground with the heel of his sandal and looked away from her.

And suddenly Nia remembered what Alun had said about

the chapel: *No one goes there — something happened — something bad!* and she suddenly found herself saying, "All right! I'll come, just for a little while!"

She could see that Emlyn was more than pleased, but trying hard not to show it. "Good!" he said. "Can I take the dog?"

Nia handed him Fly's leash. "I wanted to see the inside of your place," she said.

Emlyn grinned. "I thought I recognized you spying on us. You're Alun's sister, aren't you? You look different in all that stuff. I wasn't sure."

Nia giggled. "I nearly fell out of the car, didn't I?"

"What's going on? Why were you in jeans one minute and then beads and a funny hat the next?"

"We moved," said Nia. "'Moved with the times!' That's what my dad says."

They began to walk up the hill. Fly too hot and thirsty now to run, and Emlyn striding faster than the dog. Nia had to take little running, hopping steps in order to keep up with the boy and to avoid loose stones on the ground.

Once a van passed on the other side of the road, its engine coughing as it strained up the hill, and Fly rushed at it, barking furiously, just as she used to do when strangers passed Tŷ Llŷr.

"She doesn't like cars and that sort of thing," Nia explained breathlessly. "She wants to go home, like me. Only it isn't home anymore — the farm, I mean, where we come from."

"Where did you come from?"

"Tŷ Llŷr, on the mountain. Dad didn't like it, the work was too rough. Sheep kept dying in the winter, and Mom said the house was too small with another baby coming. But you'd think she'd want to stay, since it was her home all her life — she was even born there. Nobody wanted to stay except me and Fly. I planted flowers there. I like to watch things grow and all the colors."

"Are there a lot of you?" Emlyn inquired. He was gazing intently at Fly, and for a moment Nia wondered if he really wanted an answer.

"Seven!" she replied. "Seven children, that is, and I'm in the middle, right in the very middle. Nerys is the oldest, she's clever and quite pretty, but Catrin is beautiful. She called herself 'Kate' last year, she thought it sounded more romantic but now she's Catrin again. She plays the piano and her hair is — oh . . ." Nia sighed. "All pale yellow and floating, like . . . like ash trees."

Emlyn looked at her with interest but he said nothing, and Nia began to wonder if she'd talked too much. She'd never been able to express herself before, and she couldn't think how it had come about. They walked on in silence until they reached the pink-and-gold railings of the chapel, and all at once Nia began to feel afraid. Fly was apprehensive, too; she kept making worried rumbling noises in her throat.

It was too bright — the painted door, the colored curtains — it was like the house of gingerbread that had tempted Hansel and Gretel, and look what had become of them! *Something happened there, something bad . . .* Alun's words kept repeating themselves in her head, but Emlyn had taken her hand and was drawing her up the steps to the door!